JOURNEY TO UTOPIA

FINDING EMMA

DEVKUMAR JAYARAM

Dedicated to Humanity

Edited by
Aliza Khan
Diya Dev

ISBN : 978-1-7353152-5-6

Copyright © 2023 by Devkumar Jayaram

All rights reserved.

No part of this book may be reproduced in any form or by any electronic or mechanical means, including information storage and retrieval systems, without written permission from the author, except for the use of brief quotations in a book review.

Disclaimer

All characters, businesses, places, events and incidents in this book are either the product of the author's imagination or used in a fictitious manner. Any resemblance to actual persons, living or dead, or actual events is purely coincidental.

1

Somewhere in the Middle East

Bright sunlight shone sharply through its eyes as the pointed claws feathered the pockets of clouds. Cruising at great speed, not a single speck of dust nor an ounce of sound was met with interference, providing a source of freedom in its range. As it was flying at a tremendous force, the eagle's acute eyes found its prey at fifteen thousand feet below and began plummeting down, ripping through the clouds. As it drew closer and closer to the ground, there was a pursuit going on between two vehicles. The old Mercedes white car moving in front had shattered windows, laden with explosives in the trunk with a timer that may blow at any minute. Driving at high speeds, the driver's eyes widen, sweat dripping down his brow, slamming into everything in his path, praying to reach a target before it explodes.

Following the car, there is an armored truck with

five soldiers firing bullets. The gravel below, smothered by the tires' immense pressure, created a dusty atmosphere, making it impossible to see.

The truck eventually reached closer to the car but it was too late, the car had already reached the embassy, crashing through the front gate. The driver inside the Mercedes closed his eyes, prayed to his deity, and with his right hand trembling, pressed the trigger, exploding him and everyone within a quarter-mile radius.

Rocks pub, Downtown, New York

Drums beat with synchrony as the disco lights sprung off the walls and it's the chaos of people.

"It's time to drink Kamikaze shots" screamed Jason, smiling broadly as he waved the drink in the air, spilling some on the floor.

A recently post-graduated 28-year-old young man and his crystal blue eyes could win the heart of every woman. He was dressed in a white button-up that lay gently on his chest with casual jeans that elevated his height. He had this charismatic aura that made him the most attractive man in the bar. Rather than pursuing his career, however, he found happiness in partying at the club and flaunting his brown hair, complemented by high cheekbones and sharp jawline to oncoming women. He was the man of the night.

"Are you guys ready? 1 2 3?" and they all drank the full shot at once, and cheered as they raised their empty cups in the air. Jason waves the bartender over to fill the table with six cups of tequila.

"Here we go," Jason uttered to himself as someone began to ask about Elly.

"A breakup" one of them answered.

"What? Again??" a sigh of disappointment filled the room.

"Listen, it's a matter of being extremely interfered with in my life. Elly was too controlling for me. Plus, these shots hit differently when she's not around." Jason said while holding a shot glass of tequila in his hands.

"That's the same thing you said about Nancy, Madison, and now Elly".

"Come on Jason, your reasons aren't justified enough," said Merry, one of his friends at the bar.

"There's always another side of the story, and I don't need to explain everything in my life." said with a wavering voice, under the influence of tequila.

"That's true. Let's cheer for the third breakup of our dear friend Jason" said Merry as she raised the glass.

"To the man who manages to blame everyone in his life except himself," John added as a joke, laughing as he drowned another shot. Although, everyone knew there was a little truth in that.

"I understand your point, but relationships are meant for caring and showing a healthy possession over your partner." Abigail smiled, looking at her boyfriend and continued

"Am I right, love?" sitting next to her and Adan pulled her closer and whispered

"Yes love" and laid a soft kiss on her forehead.

"Get a room!" Jason said and he smiled with a blank expression. *I am waiting for the right girl*, he uttered to himself.

"All right, let's talk about what's for the future?" Abigail asked.

"I and Adan are relocating to Seattle. I'll be joining an international corporation next week, and Adan will find work there once we arrive," Abigail explained with great enthusiasm.

"I'll be working for my father's business, looking after the auto dealership in New Jersey," said another buddy.

"What about you Jason?"

"I'm not sure what to do. It's between political science or architecture. I need some time to figure it out" Jason replied, staring intently at the beer glass. Intrinsically there were thousands of thoughts roaming in Jason's mind- lots of questions that were left unanswered. But deep inside he knew that there must be a place or a calling that will lead him to his unsaid goal.

Brooklyn, New York

Brooklyn- a wonderful place to visit in the United States. Famous for its enchanting beauty and a place filled with extroverts on every street. Besides the mesmerizing glimpse of the famous Brooklyn Bridge to the Barclays center, there is a diverse range to visit and explore. Significantly the place is marked with appealing personalities on the road or even in the nightclubs. The best part of the city is that everyone gets a chance to shed the burden over their shoulders by partying all night.

Saturday night is there to get the soul relaxation therapy. Other than partying in Brooklyn there were some happily married couples who waited about a week to get themselves united at Saturday's dinner eve. The wooden ceilings and traditional carpet with signature lighting decor, the house seems just perfect for the dinner. The scent of lasagna was placed next to the wine on a table.

Knocking at the door. "This must be Brook." Edward commented,

Edward is an old man wearing a brown leather jacket accompanied by traditional boots and black pants. And here comes the old man named Brook with his sparkling black eyes and blonde hair with his unusual smiley face. Edward welcomed his dear friend at home. Sitting across the tables here comes a delighted conversation.

"How was your week serving the city, Brook?" Edward asked while pouring a glass of wine.

"It's always terrible, you know. What you can expect from a politician. Just paying his services around passing bills and approvals, and the cycle continues." answered in a tired tone.

"Hah! That's what life is" Edward commented while serving him a glass of wine.

"How is Jason doing?"

"Well! What can one expect from a young man who just finished post-graduation and is seeking adventure and pleasure. Leaving the hopes of his parents and future aside." responded while sipping the wine.

"You should be proud of your son; at least he graduated."

"I am proud, but what is he going to do with his Architect and political science degree?"

"A party with some politicians and a discussion about city architecture." Brook cherished with his unique humor.

Both of them knew that Jason is a brilliant man but besides his intelligence there lies the unique adventure that refrains him to stick with a particular goal. This was a long night and the conversation continued deciding Jason's future as his area of interest does not align with the ones he wants to do. The conversation continued and ended up on the fact that let Jason decide whatever he wants to do eventually he will. For years until now Jason is the only child who grew up in the limelight as the whole family believes in his exceptional talent. But here there was a milestone that keeps on scaring the family and this was the incautious nature that made him live with his parents till date as he won't find a consistent job in the town-at least according to him.

2

The sun was glaring and there was a haze in the sky. Birds were chirping and flying around the sky while enjoying the calm, peaceful air in the sky. People were murmuring on the streets and rushing towards their destination. News channels were occupied by sensational news in the city. The aura of New York City seems to be overblown where everyone emerged into their own lives while exploring the different anomalous adventures of life. A new day rises with a lot of responsibilities and fulfilling the undone work in their lives.

"What's the ti- I'm late!!!" Jason sprang out of his bed upon looking at the clock on his wall.

"Jason, are you up honey? Your dad is asking about you..." his mother said slowly, knocking at the door. There were certain conflicts going on between Jason and his father, Jason seems irresponsible and their opinions were always conflicting.

"Yeah, I know Mom. I don't want any lectures... Don't worry I'm coming."

Jason opened his cupboard and evaluated his wardrobe. He thought he should look professional rather than vague and formal. He selected a white cotton shirt with a combination of black formal pants before he went to the bathroom and takes a shower. While seeing himself in the bathroom mirror he was unable to recognize himself. Thoughts circled in his mind about the first day at his new job and his future plan, to be the richest and most powerful man so that he could afford whatever he wants in his life and not be dependent on others, especially his parents. While he was still staring at the mirror a noise came from the door.

"Jason, honey what are you doing in the bathroom? Why are you taking so much time there?"

" I can't even take a shower in peace......" Jason burbled.

"Hurry up."

His mother went straight into the kitchen to prepare breakfast for her son and husband. Meanwhile, Edward was sitting while reading the magazine and looking at the clock while comprehending his son's careless, ignorant attitude and dealing with his inner thoughts that were wrapped up with internal conflicts.

"It seems preposterous to me. It's the first day of his new Job and he is still here..." Edward was making grotesque comments about his own son due to his careless attitude.

"At least, he started trying and taking the initial steps of his career....Stop discouraging our son" Ella said while making a gloomy face as she was always stuck between her son and husband.

In the meantime, Jason got ready and stood in front of the mirror. While he was reminiscing his childhood full of thrill without the hint of agitation related to his life. Throwing a bicycle on the lawn after coming from high school and slouched into his room. Turning on the computer and playing games while resolving the puzzles in the meantime connected with his friends on discord. Listening to his father's grotesque comments made Jason jaded and lacking enthusiasm in his life. While remembering his childhood playing games, he tucked in his shirt, put on a tie, and wrapped up himself with droplets of perfume, the fragrance that will complement his personality. He rushed downstairs for breakfast and for the meeting with his own parents.

"Mom, I think I should have breakfast in the office. I should be on time today otherwise it would be a terrible situation for me."

"It's totally bizarre...Isn't it? You should be responsible enough to manage your time otherwise you would be jeopardizing this job as well...." Edward remarked while eating his breakfast.

Jason listened to him while his blood was boiling up after listening to his father but he rather ignored it and slumped down into memory lane. Where his childhood friend Austin tells him the short therapy for relaxation...

"Breathe in and out, Jason....breathe in and out and let it go.."

Austin was his childhood friend who was always there when Jason was in the skepticism phase of his life. He had full red cheeks, and round eyes, and was fair in color. In the front of Austin's teeth, a tooth was chipped just enough for it to be noticed. Austin loved to wear a hoodie as he often found comfort in it and hid his insecurities from others, he always loved to watch superheroes. But circumstances snatched Jason's friend and his childhood from him.

Jason escalated his speed and went straight out of the house heading towards his office. While going through his lawn he saw Mrs. Grace watering her plants. An old lady that was attached to Jason for years from his childhood. Her white hair represented her age that was being terminated with time, her white skin was converted into a brownish tone, round big eyes with a hint of brightness in her eyes, wearing an elongated white frock that was complimenting her soft tone of voice.

"Good to see you, Mrs. Grace. Hope you are good at taking shots at this age as well...."Jason greeted as he ordered his cab.

"Jason I owe you many for these...Where are you heading by the way in the early morning? Did Edward throw you out." Grace chuckled slightly while using her weak sense of humor.

"Following some unknown path, while figuring out the reason for my existence ...Consider it for now Mrs. Grace. Will see you in the evening." he sat in the Cab while saying goodbye to Mrs. Grace and her little cute puppy.

While in the cab, he was evaluating the hustle and bustle of the city and he thought that this crowd is the major essence of this lively city. Jason and the cab driver started negotiating about different aspects of their lives. The cab driver told him that he did his degree in engineering and he was a highly qualified person. Jason was stunned after hearing him and the main question started revolving around his mind.

How did he end up here... Jason inquired to himself.

"What are you thinking, sir?" the cab driver asked

"Why didn't you go for the Job- if you don't mind me asking..."

"Well, I did go for the Job and I worked in the IT department of a software company for 6 years of my life. But the most important factor that a person seeks during his job is massive respect from his coworkers, managers, HOD, and from the whole department. And I missed the respect in my company and that led me to quit my job and ended up here. Every man does not fall into the category of working for other people and can compromise in terms of their respect. So, I decided to start my own business and in the meantime, I'm driving the cab."

"I'm sorry... every person deserves respect and you are doing a great job. I'm really happy that you have the insight and are thinking about starting your own business. Best wishes for your new business venture." He wished as he paid the fare and exited the car.

While walking Jason was looking at the sky while evaluating the building of his company. "World Press Corporation" is written at the top of the building and the title of the company has been enlightened with the mesmerizing light that gives a professional outlook of the company. It was a huge media company comprising 35 floors. Each level features gorgeous, tranquil rooms as well as many cafeterias and meeting rooms. The building was tall, rectangular in shape made up of blue glass for its exterior representation. Around the building, there was a courtyard on all four sides from where cars entered and exited to the parking lot situated in the basement. The interior of the building was built with white tiles and gives a serene professional environment.

Jason entered the building while evaluating the crystal glass infrastructure of the office. While walking inside the building, he noticed that he was walking on a soft and mushy platform surrounded by a crowd. Jason was a bit confused, and flustered due to his first day at the office. His hands were in his pockets and headed straight towards the receptionist. While dealing with his agitation he confirmed the conference room for the new bunch of batches orientation that was joining the company.

"It is located on the 32nd floor. Room 202, sir. Best

wishes on your first day." The receptionist informed Jason and directed him toward the elevator.

Jason entered the lift and reached the 32nd floor while portraying positive gestures to the staff of the company. He reached the door of the room and he was perplexed. His heartbeat was fluctuating and his facial expressions were deviating from the normal scale. He closed his eyes and inhaled the air while taking a deep breath. While counting from 1 to 10 he snarled into the room. A big room on the topmost floor of the company with a grayish interior, carpet flooring, and double folding glass doors. The big table and professional chairs were placed just in front of the wide window and in the middle of the room. While seeing through the windows of the room it was exhibiting the view of the city outside in an aesthetically pleasing way with a touch of nature. Jason entered the room while giving positive gestures to the bunch of people and introducing himself while telling them about his name.

"You must be Jason...right?" Ben asked him. He was the HR manager of the department and organized this whole orientation.

"Yeah........."

"Great. Welcome to our company Jason. We are delighted to have you and other new members in our company. Have a seat and we will be proceeding in a few minutes."

Jason greeted everyone and in the right corner of the table, there were two seats that were available. Jason went there and sat down. While he was evaluating the whole room and circulating in his own chair, something seemed bizarre to Jason. As he was missing something in this room. He started ruminating while using his keen eyes. There was the blurry illusion of the person that was dragging Jason and developing curiosity in him while listening to his voice. In his inner self, he started questioning why he was so curious about the person and unable to see his face because he was leaning back and his face was in another corner of the room. Jason, due to his cumbersome curiosity, stood from his chair and with a fake representation started walking towards the dispenser for drinking water. While drinking water from his mug, he saw the face of the person and was stunned after seeing his face. His eyes became watery, his emotions were fluctuating as he missed something from his entire life and suddenly someone was there.

"I can't believe that he is here....but how?" Jason mumbled.

3

This was Austin, Jason's old buddy-the one he's been thinking that he had loosened long ago. Time flies and Austin has to move to another city in the US due to his parent's job within those years Jason never heard of Austin. This was the sharply pointed nose with spectacularly glared brown eyes complementing his sharp jawline along with his pale skin. But things have changed. The pitch of his voice was quite high. Jason was only able to recognize him by his sharp jawline as no one either possessed that spectacular feature. Jason was quite shocked by his presence. He was standing still in his blank state of mind, and at the same time, the whole conference room was packed by newcomers. Everything in the room was quite new and somewhat strange for him but most importantly there was Austin.

There was a loud chatter in the conference room and everyone in the room seemed quite optimistic except the existing employees. They were all sitting in the right row of the conference hall while men wearing black and blue suits with formal ties and some women wearing black skirts with high heels. While on the other side, there were a bunch of new employees who were as excited as a teenager excited for the first day at high school except Jason who was just sitting right opposite from Austin and watching him with a scent of recognition.

Meanwhile, Emma, a young woman, entered the conference room. Jason's gaze was pulled to her right away. his heart started pounding fast, and began to feel immense feelings for her. Her smile was enticing, and Jason was unable to comprehend his feelings but he knew there was some deep connection that he couldn't explain, it was a love at first sight. He later recognized that while she was in the same neighborhood as where he had grown up and that he had frequently seen her but never talked to her, they were both residing in quite different realities.

The HR made a request to be silent as the directors are approaching to give a basic Introduction about the company and the respective roles. There was still chattering in the room but by now the intensity of the whole cross-conversation was settled to some extent.

Two males in casual dress entered the room. As they entered the room there was a deathly silence. This was Paul and Mike. Mike was a director and Paul was his boss who was the executive vice president of the company, they both were in fact the most crucial pillars of the company. The conference began and the spotlight of the whole scene was Mr. Paul and Mr. Mike. They explained every single bit of the essential information to the crew. The whole room seems quite energetic as there was not a single moment to lose interest. And finally, the whole presentation ended and everyone was clear about the mission statement of the company and how things function in the company's atmosphere. And here comes a big round of a clause for the presenters and their team for presenting such a tremendous and useful piece of information for the whole team. Mike asked everyone to introduce themselves one after the other so that there will be a colossal interaction between the existing and new employees. Meanwhile, everyone was giving their introduction, Jason was quite mesmerized by the fact that his efforts made fruit but there was rising concern about Austin – the childhood buddy sitting at one corner of the conference room chatting with team members and on the other end, he saw Emma trying to adjust to the new atmosphere.

As Jason approached Austin to initiate conversation, Austin turned to look at who was approaching and was equally astounded to see him. He immediately recognized him but was not quite sure.

"Are you Jason…" in a confusing way Austin asked?

"Of course buddy" he moved his hand in a gesture that only Austin recognizes.

He was speechless for a moment and later they both shook hands and hugged each other.

"So how's your life going?"

"Well, it's going great. How about you, buddy?" he raised his voice and went closer to Jason.

"Well, a roller coaster ride, if you know what I mean." He chuckled "Where have you been?"

"A long story my friend "- Austin replied and made a quiet laugh.

After a period of time they were together and here began a never-ending conversation of the childhood mates. The conversation begins with a quiet smile and then it turns to be a rollercoaster of laughter, and happiness painted by thousands of good memories. Things might seem different but deep inside they were the same just like old days when they were ten-year-old Jason and Austin ran back to home after school and picked up fresh apples from the nearest neighborhood with a sharp run to the memories of secretly painting the school's wall and the whole complaint story.

By now the place was filled with pleasant memories of their childhood but there was still a void that took those precious years away from them. The chatters continued Sipping the hot cup of latte and Jason was making odd facial expressions. The behavior of Jason brings back memories of his odd facial expressions in the past when he was curious about anything.

Austin just grinned and stated "Jason! You are still the same", he chuckled.

Jason nodded his head followed by a huge smile. Austin and Jason were discussing the company's members since everything was new to them. While they were conversing, Emma stepped in front of them, and Austin detected a potential lover's scent in the room. Jason had a big smile on his face and was blushing.

The HR interfered in the hall and told the crowd that it is customary that the director arranges a diverse range of competitions, one that aims to identify the spectacular skills of the employees at the company. Jason secretly eavesdrops on the conversation and was just getting himself clear over the whole scenario.

Meanwhile, there was an echo in the room-this was Mike.

"Everyone please get yourselves arranged in the middle of the great hall. There's an announcement"

Everyone in the room followed the instructions and got themselves arranged in the middle of the great hall.

"As we all knew that there are emerging talents who have just joined us at the firm. We pay them a warm welcome." Mike added with joy in his tone. His words were followed by great clapping and positive gestures. Later he throws a big surprise to the newcomers.

"Let's start our journey with an amazing game that we usually conduct with newcomers."

"What game?" There was chattering and humming among the crowd.

He announces a competition in order to get trained as a news reporter. Basically, he asks everyone to pick each other to form a group of 3, everyone starts selecting each other, of course, Jason and Austin were together already, and they need one additional partner, Jason suggested we should include Emma.

"I knew you were going to say that," Austin responded with a smile.

They approached Emma and introduced themselves, Jason slowly revealed who he was and have seen Emma quite often in the neighborhood. Surprisingly Emma also knew Jason but had never spoken.

"I've seen you many times but never knew your name, nor we spoke" Emma responded.

"We were in our own world I guess" responded with his soft voice and smile. Her charismatic looks and vibes attracted Jason like a magnet which he never experienced before while dating other girls in his past, there was something in Emma.

All three had a long conversation and in the meantime, everyone formed a group, there were 4 groups in total.

"We have placed 2 hidden maps in the hall and you will have to hunt down those maps," Mike told the group

There was chatter among the group "Where can it be? How are we gonna do it?" And the list of questions prolongs.

"Silence please, work with your teammates to find the maps, you have 15 mins and the time starts now" Mike added

As soon as the timer clicks in there was a great

dissonance in the hall. As expected each of the team climbed towards the crowded corner of the hall searching for the map. And here one after the other the teams were madly in search of maps. While Austin, Jason, and Emma were standing right in the middle of the hallway. Jason asked Austin if he had any clue about the game. Unintentionally, Emma answered saying how these games are set to access the skill set of the new employees.

"We have to think differently." Austin and Jason replied at the same time.

"Come let's approach the stage"

Just like the old days, Austin said to himself. Standing right on the stage the three of them began to observe the whole hall and there came a huge shout in the room.

"We have found a map!" That was Matt, Jessica, and Steve. Still, there were 10 min left and Jason's team was standing empty-handed.

Emma stepped forward and added.

"I think we should start looking for the map -let's get into the battlefield" she mocked.

"I think Jason knows exactly what to do," Austin replied.

Let's get back to childhood misery. Austin replied and they looked at each other with a huge smile on their face. In their childhood, they used to hide things that went just normal to everyone. The place that won't catch any of the sights. And here it goes Austin asked Emma to search the doorways, and entrance along with exit halls. Emma and Jason went to search down the places, and as expected, Emma found a decorative map among the side decors at the entrance.

"Time's up!" Mike made a sharp reminder.

Luckily both the maps were found and Matt's team won the competition. On a safer note, Jason's team was second and the other 2 teams lost.

"Well, this was a test to see how well you trust, communicate, and build relationships within your team" Mike replied and handed over 2 more maps to the lost team.

"Now the real work begins. Each team will take that map and find a story in that particular area and report back. Each week's winning story will be featured in a news article. Also, the team who found the map first will have the option to choose the map that they are interested in from other teams if they want to" MIke announced.

Here comes a twist knowing that Jason's team was quite happy with their locations for news coverage. The evil Jessica demanded the location of Jason's team, since they were number 1 in finding the map, they had the upper hand in choosing the location they were interested in. Austin was quite upset but at the same time, he was happy that Jason & Emma were with him. But a new task is ahead of them. Competition is quite hard and it's still hard to evaluate which team will have the best story.

4

The next morning, Mike and Paul were inside the room discussing the embassy incident. They briefly discussed the incident with each other. The time arrived when all the teams are supposed to get out of the workstation, go out and cover some sizzling news. Meanwhile, Matt and his teammates came forward to talk to each other. Matt greeted Jason in quite an awkward manner.

"So, Jason huh, I hope you and your team are in good hands. Don't forget, this is a competition and not just a casual game of any kind, and we will give you a hard time."

Jason stared at him and felt uneasy about his aggressiveness; he had never met Matt before, so he smiled and said, "Cool down buddy, we don't need to murder anyone or anything."

On hearing this Matt gave a strange laugh and said, "It looks like Jason does not have the passion to become the best reporter, remember only one best team will lead, and that would be ours."

On hearing all of this conversation, Jason told him that they will see who would win, he went to his teammates Austin and Emma, spoke about news coverage, and headed towards that location.

They finally reached the park. They were in an odd situation, as Jason had told them what Matt had said to him. The situation had become tense. Emma was wearing a white colored t-shirt and her cheeks have gotten red due to anger at Matt. Austin looked at her and realized that she was angry.

"You all are going to lose, but don't worry I'll give you some leftover pizza at our party once we win." Austin imitated Jessica while bumping into her in the cafeteria.

On listening to Austin doing so both Emma and Jason burst into laughter and it eased the moment. They were debating what they should and should not cover. Meanwhile, Emma was evaluating the whole area around them and suddenly something took her attention. Emma looked around and pointed at someone.

"Hey guys look over there, it seems that I might have found our first story...." Emma pointed at a girl and an elderly couple.

A lovely elderly couple was contemplating crossing the street; the woman was using a walker, and the man was supporting her shoulder. However, the road was crowded with moving vehicles and nobody was stopping to allow the pair to pass. A little girl nearby was swinging on a set of swings when she saw the couple. She rushed towards them to help them to cross the road. Emma was observing the girl and felt it was wonderful that the little girl had stopped having fun when she spotted the couple suffering and had rushed to help them. Jason and Austin started looking at the girl and he rolled down his camera and started to film the whole incident. While the little girl was helping the couple cross the road, they heard a few voices from the swings. A woman who was almost 30 years old was shouting;

"Maria where did you go, Maria?" She was quite upset. She was looking for her daughter with her friend, with whom she was talking before. Emma understood that Maria is her little girl, she shouted,

"Look at the road, Maria is there." As soon as she said that, her mother turned around and saw Maria helping the old aged couple by holding their hands and walking with them down the road. She stopped the cars by pointing her hands and finally helped them in crossing the road. The whole incident was filmed by Austin. A man was standing above his balcony and was looking at Maria helping the couple. He immediately came down with a teddy bear in his hands. He handed over the teddy bear to Maria while saying,

"You're a very good girl. You showed an act of kindness and it never goes unrewarded. Here you go."

The girl held the teddy bear and her face glowed.

She ran joyfully towards her mother and said, "Mommy, look, I received a teddy bear."

Her mother gave her a bear hug and broke down in tears.

Jason, Austin, and Emma were also smiling. They knew that no one has seen such reports in months, therefore it will help them to publish this weekly news and will spread a positive vibe around.

While on the other hand, other teams were also looking out for certain stories. Matt and his team Jessica and Steve were still looking around as they were not just looking for any normal story, but they were looking for some sizzling story that will help them to get their story more than everyone else. They were quite passionate about winning and setting high hopes. They arrived at a store where cops were already collecting evidence of an incident. Matt and Jessica found it a suitable point to dig a sensational story. Both of them scattered and started questioning the witnesses who were there during the incident. Matt looked at the injured man who was shot and was bleeding badly. He was not in his senses as the bullet had crossed his left side close to his heart. Matt went to a man standing next to him and started to question him.

"Hello, my name is Matt from World News Corporation, and I'll be covering this incident here. Can you tell me what happened here?"

The man said that he came into the store to buy a few groceries for dinner. He was shopping when he heard a pitched voice, as he turned around, he saw a man who was drunk, his eyes were red, scattered hair, his lips, and nose were covered, but it was quite obvious that he was not in his senses. He pointed his revolver at the shopkeeper and demanded that he hand over all of his money. The shopkeeper tried to calm him down, but he threatened to shoot him and demanded that he give away his mobile and other possessions. The shopkeeper tried to be smart and went down to pick up his gun. The robber saw him doing that, he instantly fired his gun, grabbed all the money from the cash counter, and ran out of the shop.

Matt and Jessica went to other witnesses of the crime scene for covering the coverage. Some of the witnesses were so terrified and perplexed due to the crime scene that their memory started fading away and they were unable to sketch the whole crime scene as it happened. However, Matt and Jessica covered every aspect of the crime scene and how it affected other people around the environment. While on the other hand, the NYPD was investigating the whole crime scene.

After a few days, Austin had a friend who had informed him of a good story. His friend is a homeless person and he told him that there are almost 2000 homeless people in the city, and they can go talk to them and cover a good story. The next day Jason and Austin drove the car to pick up Emma from her house. Jason texted her to come out of the house as they were waiting outside, Austin was observing facial expressions of Jason as if something fishy was going on inside his mind.

"Dude, Are you okay?" inquired with great curiosity

"Ofcourse, what's wrong with me"

"She will come here soon. You kept on looking at her door as if she was misplaced somewhere..." commented with a sarcastic smile.

"Come on, buddy, we're going to be late, and she has to come quickly...."

Austin started to know that Jason had feelings for Emma. Meanwhile, their conversation erupted as Emma sat inside the car. They went straight to cover their new story, as this will be a different story from the previous one.

They reached the destination where they found numerous people living in a camp with poor hygiene and dirty clothes and rotten shoes. The place was full of stories. They went to a middle-aged man, who was married and had two children. He had a little girl who was 6 years and a boy who was 10 years old. The man had a family but he did not have any source of income to support them. They were living in a small camp together. They started to interview him, Jason and Emma were voice recording it while Austin was taking photographs and making small videos. All of them were busy, as they knew that this report was going to make them stand out, and they were certain to win the competition.

The man used to have a good life. His children

Journey to Utopia

used to go to good schools and they had every necessity of life. They used to live in a beautiful 4 bedroom house and were living their best life. But the circumstances were not in their favor. The man had bought health insurance which was supposed to support him and his family in the tones of difficulty. He purchased it by looking at its benefits but he did not pay attention to the details of insurance and accepted it without studying it completely. Unfortunately, her wife got sick badly and needed to be hospitalized. After being hospitalized her bills were paid by the insurance. But only 60 percent of the bills were paid by the insurance, the rest was supposed to be taken care of by the man himself which took all of his savings.

The economic condition of the country became worse and many people lost their jobs, including him on contrary, he couldn't keep up his mortgage and lost his house as well. The conditions became harsh, but luckily her wife's sister asked them to live with them for the time being. They moved in and lived with her for a few months. But the conditions became harsh and they started to have certain fights until they had to leave her house. It was the time when they started to live on the streets. In the beginning, it was so much more difficult, but after living for few months, they have become accustomed to it. The man said, now it has become impossible for him to find a job as he is living off the streets, they do not have any home address, nor does he have any suitable clothing for an interview. They eat at night quite hard with the earnings collected by them off the streets.

The whole team was shaken by the story. They were not expecting to meet such a skilled man who went to live off the streets with his little children. Emma and Jason would look at each other with hopelessness and were empathetic hearing their story. In the meanwhile, his two beautiful children came to Austin with paper airplanes. Austin looked at them and sat down with them. He asked them to bring more paper, and with that, he taught them how to make caps and boats out of paper.

After completing the interview, Emma handed over some money and promised to help them in the future. Later, the team came out of their camp and were having an awkward silence for some time. Emma had not felt like this before, She could not digest how a good-earning family was made to live off the streets. She found so many flaws in the insurance and banking industry. But Jason was a person who took it lightly and was not serious about the situation, he was still in a competitive mindset and his main aim was to win against Matt and his team.

"This would be our best news to win," Jason responded.

"Are you serious, you are still thinking about winning, didn't their story touch your heart," Emma stated

"I know Emma but this is reality, come out of the

perfect world that you are looking for, you are not going to see it."

Austin was quietly hearing their conversation without interfering in between.

Emma became angry and shouted at Jason "You should get serious sometimes, and pay close attention to your life as well, otherwise you would end up losing many things."

Jason looked at Emma and did not know how to react. He could not say a word, since he didn't know Emma well.

There was silence for a while, and Emma eventually recognized that she didn't know Jason well and shouldn't have responded to him in that way.

Few days had passed, another team, Suzy, and her teammate learned that there had been an incident of racism in a certain area of the city. They went there and began interrogating a woman who had seen the event. Suzy urged his teammate to record the interview.

"Can you tell me what happened here? " Suzy asked the lady

The lady started saying " I stepped out of my store for a cigarette and observed that it was dark and that an Asian couple was approaching from one end of the sidewalk and a black man was coming from the other side. The couple noticed that he was approaching them and they became tensed, he came in front of them and requested for their assistance since he had misplaced his phone and needed to contact his family members. The pair assumed the individual was there to harm them and there was a burst of loud noises as the Asian woman screamed for aid. As he had done nothing, the man began to challenge them about their actions. He began explaining his good intentions, but they didn't believe him, were scared, and contacted the cops. The cops arrived on the spot and began investigating."

Suzy started speaking in front of the camera "Thank you miss, you see, the world is surrounded by both good,bad and confused people. And sometimes life indulged in the darkest phase of our lives where we didn't know how to deal with the malicious darkness in our lives and we were wrapped in our wrong perceptions about individuals. This is Suzy from World New Channel."

The team covered their stories and they left that place.

Few days later, it was an exciting time for all teams to bring their cover stories in front of Mike and Paul so that they could pick the best story for publication or to air on their News channel.

Each team presented the story they covered at Mike's office. Following an internal discussion between Mike and Paul, a meeting was called in the conference room, and requested all teams to join in order to determine which story was the best for weekly news.

Everyone believed that their narrative would be published, and they all appeared to be quite enthusiastic.

5

Mike started speaking "We are really delighted to have you all here. I must say that all the teams did well and some of you had turbulence in your emotions. I congratulate you all for your hard work and best efforts. And I really hope in the coming months you all will cover more interesting news.... I now announce that Matt and Suzy's teams have the best new coverage which will be considered for airing this coming week " Mike shared his views while addressing the whole conference room and went to his room.

Emma was shocked upon listening to the results but Austin and Jason did not seem to look worried at all, She could not keep it to herself and went to Mike directly. She asked him why their story was not selected.

Mike responded "People don't listen to stories of compassion; they want stories about tragedy, murder, agony, bigotry, and so on. Only such stories get renowned; next time you should focus on such stories since no one wants to hear about acts of kindness or poverty. The better a news organization's consumer rating, the more advertisements it will run and the higher the amount clients will pay for 30-second or 1-hour time slots. You should focus more on consumer mindsets, behaviors, and expectations. This industry will not embrace your narrative of kindness or sympathy."

She walked out of his office with a sorrowful heart, but Jason seemed unconcerned, he showed no consideration for Emma's feelings.

The day went off and everyone reached their homes. It was the middle of the night, and Jason was in deep thought. He was thinking about his past relationship; he broke up with his girlfriend right before joining the company. He had not taken anything so seriously yet in his life. Despite their philosophical differences, he had a soft spot for Emma; he saw her as unique from other females and felt a connection with her. He thought to himself that Emma has a strong view about how she wants to live her life, that she is a passionate person, and that she is unlike anybody else who lives solely for weekends and parties. He reasoned that it would be a good idea to ask her out on a date, even if it was just two coworkers having lunch together. He wasn't sure if Emma was looking at him like that. As a result, he decided to ask her out and see what happens. Slowly, his eyes began to close as he thought about her, and fell asleep.

The alarm continued to sound the next morning, but Jason snoozed and slept until the alarm rang again, at which point he awoke. He checked the time and hurried to get dressed. He arrived at the workplace late, and after finishing his work, Jason asked Emma if they could have dinner together.

Emma said yes right away, and they headed to a nearby restaurant. Jason ordered a burger, while Emma got pasta. They kept chatting about the office, their families, and their friends. Emma informed her that her old friend Myra was getting married in India and that she intends to go. Jason looked delighted by the trip and requested if he can accompany her to India. Emma hesitated at first but eventually accepted. Jason was relieved that he would get to know her better when they traveled to another continent together. They confirmed their trip to India over dinner.

The next morning Jason went to Austin's desk and told him that they had planned to go to India and it would be fun if he could join as well. He had heard so many things about Indian culture, food, and weddings, but Austin did not show any interest as he had other plans.

Later Emma and Jason went to Mike's office to ask for a vacation. On listening to the idea of going to India, Mike asked them, "Why don't you work in India instead of taking a vacation? India is a rich, cultural country, and the company needs more stories regarding different countries. Plus, going there to a wedding is the best time to explore and write about it."

Emma and Jason became quite excited about this idea and the trip.

"Wow... I cannot believe I am going to attend Myra's wedding and it is also going to be a professional trip. I cannot wait to get my packing done." Emma stated,

Jason looked at her and nodded."All right, then, I'll book the tickets."

Emma said ok, Jason booked the tickets for the last week of the month.

The day came when they were traveling to India, and all their bags were packed. Austin came to pick them up and he dropped them at the airport.

"Have a safe flight, see you both, have fun, and don't forget to share some photos." Austin hugged both of them while talking.

He pulled Jason to a side and gave him a sarcastic look and told "This is your opportunity dude". and drove off in his car.

They both went inside the airport and boarded the plane.

6

They were having a nice time on the flight, talking about their childhoods and sharing stories with one other.

Jason just glared outside the window and stated. "Wow, just look at that sky! It's so beautiful"

"It really is. I love how the colors are changing as the sun sets" Emma responded.

"Yeah, it's amazing how the sky can look so different at different times of the day. The clouds look like they're made of cotton candy"

"I know, right? They're so fluffy and soft-looking. I almost want to reach out and touch them."

"It's funny how when we're on the ground, we don't really pay much attention to the sky. But up here, it's like a whole different world."

"Absolutely. It's like we're floating in a sea of clouds."

As the plane soared high above the clouds, they

both couldn't help but marvel at the stunning view before them.

The flight finally landed in Mumbai, India, after a 16-hour journey. They came out of the airport and started to look for Myra. Instead, they found a man holding a board with Emma's name on it. It was Krish, Myra's brother. They greeted him and he asked them to join him in the car as he would be taking them to his house. Emma and Jason picked up their luggage and loaded it in the trunk of his car.

Emma was too excited to meet Myra, "I cannot wait to meet her after such a long time."

"She is also waiting for you, dear Emma," Krish replied with a smile.

Krish drove them to his house. Mumbai's streets appeared to be fairly crowded, with too much traffic, Emma and Jason were worried since so many people were breaking the law. Some animals were wandering between the lanes of cars, motorcycles, rickshaws and several vehicles passed in the incorrect direction while they were stuck in the congested town. They both had the chance to view Mumbai's slums in greater detail as they drove, It was crowded with people and cottages close to each other. Emma was shocked to see this location. After some time, they started to see high-rise buildings.

Jason commented, "it seems like this part of town was a blend of slums and high-rise buildings."

Krish laughed, "This is common in major cities. let me educate you a little about our culture."

He told them India is the 2nd most populous country in the world. It has numerous ethnicities, and people speak various languages here. The food is amazing in India and marriages are one of the biggest event for any family. He told them that they would enjoy themselves a lot at Myra's wedding. He showed people who were eating street food, which was widespread and popular.

"Take some rest and enjoy the event tonight. One of these days, I'll take you both out to see Mumbai and explore some good cuisine."

Emma asked Krish that she had heard a lot about the spiritual masters in India.

"Yes, you have heard exactly right, there are so many masters and yogis here, I can take you to meet a few if you are interested."

"Yes, I would love to. We could write about them in our article, what do you think Jason?" Jason nodded his head. He seemed quite happy about coming to India with her, so he was just agreeing with whatever she was saying.

They reached their destination. It was a beautiful big bungalow that was decorated so beautifully with flowers and posters. The entrance had a big poster of the bride and groom's picture with writing: Myra weds Raj.

They stepped out of the car. Myra was waiting for them, and as soon as she saw the car Myra rushed toward Emma and hugged her. She started to cry a little, it was a heart-touching and beautiful moment.

Myra introduced Emma to her family, her father, mother, cousins, and sisters. Both of them had so much to talk about as they were meeting after so many years. She took Emma and Jason to their room. She asked them to get some rest, as they would be soon attending the Sangeet function in the evening. Weddings are one of the most important ceremonies in Indian culture, and they often span 3 to 7 days.

Myra brought Emma a gorgeous Salwar Kameez outfit to wear when she freshened herself, and Krish brought Jason a kurta pajama garment as well. They dressed up in exquisite Indian attire. Emma wore bright, gold earrings along with them, taking some amazing pictures after. They were enjoying the party, especially the Sangeet function. The hall was packed with friends, cousins, and family members of the bride. Myra introduced Emma to her future husband. The functions had started and people were dancing. to numerous Bollywood signature songs. The dinner was served and they got to enjoy various dishes and especially Sarson ka Saag (curry) and Roti (Indian bread). Emma found Indian food exotic since she liked spicy foods, however, Jason had difficulty eating hot and his cheeks were all red, he couldn't handle that much spice. Later, they had Lassi, and ice cream which cooled him down a bit. They were enjoying the function the most. Seeing so many people at a wedding was so unique for Jason and Emma. They had so many paternal and maternal uncles & aunt, cousins, their brothers, and sisters. Everyone was dancing and cheering for the bride and groom. There was so much love in the air. Emma felt good as she saw people talking to each other with so much love and care. Everyone was included in the dances, they made sure that no one was feeling left out. In the end, the cousins started to dance around the bride and groom and cheered them on. Emma and Jason were touched by seeing so much love and passion there.

After dancing Jason sat down at a table. He saw a little boy who was not having any fun but he was cleaning the tables. The boy was around ten years of his age. Jason found it quite strange for such a little boy to work at a wedding. Krish came to the table and brought some beers.

He noticed that Jason was looking at the boy. He told him that there is a lot of poverty in India, and there are numerous people who started to work at a very early age. Parents bring their children with them to work, to get them paid as well. Such people do not go to school and start to work quite early.

After a while, Jason and Emma were talking to Myra & Krish, they were telling her that they were quite happy to be there.

"I want to see the Taj Mahal," Emma said, "and since I'm here, may we go?"

"Why not, we still have time for the wedding, we can travel tomorrow, we could leave for Delhi in the morning, drive to Agra to see the Taj Mahal, and return in the night," Krish said.

Emma was so excited that she asked Jason to be

ready early in the morning. Jason agreed to do so. They made plans to visit the Taj Mahal.

The next morning everyone woke up around 4 am and left for the airport. The flight took off at 5 am and landed at 6 am in Delhi. They came out of the airport and the whole area was covered in fog.

"Wow, it appears to be nice weather; fog has totally enveloped the entire region." Jason made a remark.

"Do not get too excited Jason and Emma, I would suggest that you two should cover your face using a mask, as this is not just fog, but chemicals suspended in the environment."

On listening to it Emma and Jason seem concerned. Jason asked them what the reason behind this smog is. Krish explained that it is because of so many factors. Although Delhi is the capital of India yet it is also one of the highest polluted cities in the world. The use of vehicles, the chemicals coming out from industries, and many other factors have contributed to the accumulation of smog in the air. This is why the city has been facing numerous issues like health problems and allergic reactions. Many people have developed certain allergic issues relating to asthma, eyes, and respiratory tract. Most of the problems occur in winter when these particles become suspended in the air like smog. Although now certain steps are being taken to control the environment, the limits of pollution have been exceeded.

They covered themselves with face masks and started to explore the city. Krish took them nearby to enjoy an amazing breakfast of Chole Batura with some spices in it. Jason took his first bite and shouted,

"Oh wow, this is amazing. I've never eaten this before, this is so good, and what do you think of it, Emma?" Emma looked at him and laughed saying that no doubt Indian food is so good. After having breakfast Krish took them to visit some important tourist points nearby. They went to the red fort and explored it. They then headed to the Lotus Temple. Jason and Emma liked the temple's splendor and that they felt at ease there. After touring these locations, they sat down to rest and ate a cube of Gola Ganda, a soft ice-like dessert. It was shaved with different syrups and dry fruit and blended with condensed milk. They loved the treat. Later, they started their journey toward Agra. It was a long 4 hour drive. They explored different points while driving, took some photographs, and noted down certain points while exploring the small town in between their journey.

After 4 hours they finally reached their destination. It was love at first sight for Emma. She was so mesmerized by the beautiful building and the atmosphere seemed so calm and romantic to her. Emma told Jason that a King built it in remembrance of his love. She showed that she was so intrigued by such love. She expressed that she would like someone to do something so special for her, slightly looking at Jason. Jason started smiling and grabbed her hand to pull her to take pictures. Krish told them that it has been nominated as a UNESCO World Heritage Site in 1983. Since then, people from all parts of the world visit it when they come to India. They hired a guide who guided them throughout their stay at the Taj Mahal. He told them that the architecture is one of its finest from the Indo-Islamic times of the sub-continent. Taj Mahal has been repaired and taken care of since then, as it has become a sign of true love and romance itself.

After enjoying a memorable trip, taking so many pictures, and noting down important points for their article they headed towards the airport in Mumbai. When they got to Mumbai, Krish started driving back home. They came to a stop at a traffic light. A little girl around 8 to 9 years old came to the car and knocked at the window. She was holding beautiful red roses. When Emma saw her, her eyes immediately filled with happiness. She lowered the window and bought all of the roses. She gave her all the cash she had, along with some chocolates.

The little girl glowed up and ran towards her mother who was also selling flowers on the other side of the road. Jason was also intrigued by seeing this. He asked Krish "what's the economic condition of India". He asked Krish.

"Here there is a lot of economic inequality in the country, either we find too rich people or too poor people who are unable to eat properly three times a day." Krish explained further, "The wealth of the top ten percent of the population accounts for 70-80% of the country's wealth, and it is growing as a result of capitalism and inheritance. The labor workforce has been revolutionized by technology and industrialization, with skilled workers earning more money than unskilled people. Wages are not spread fairly across the population. People at the top earn 20 to 50 times more than poor people who are dependent on daily wages. Also, on the other hand, technological advancements that lead to automation have resulted in job losses in many areas, and as you are aware, we are the world's most populated country, which means that finding a job becomes difficult due to competition and less vacancy, people must find other ways to make a living."

"Oh, I understand, then why are some poor children not sent to school? Isn't it mandatory in this country? Or is there anything else that I'm missing" Jason asked

"It's not mandatory here, the majority of the children go to school and prefer private schools because of the high academic standards, even though the private school tuition is expensive. But the rest who are not able to afford it will go to a government or private-aided school. The learning standards, infrastructure, and management of government schools are so bad that children's enthusiasm for learning is low. Also, many families' incomes are so low that they must rely on daily wages; as a result, they are unable to send their children to school. Instead of sending them to schools, they send them to work to support their family." Krish explained this to him in detail.

"Wow......In the United States, education is free

and compulsory for all children until they reach the 12th grade. Something similar should be done here as well.."

"To do so, we must first eliminate corruption, raise education standards in government schools to the point where they can be comparable to private schools, and people pay taxes on a regular basis, and a portion of that tax money should go to school, allowing free education to everyone."

They had arrived home by then, and there was a Mehandi ceremony going on, everyone was chatting and enjoying the beautiful night. They dressed up in traditional attire for the ritual.

Emma and Jason rushed up and got ready. Everyone was scrutinizing each other's dresses, enjoying the ceremony. According to the customs they wrapped up the ceremony along with the dance competitions and everyone headed towards their homes and rooms after attending the event. Jason and Emma evaluate the customs of India and imprint them in their minds so that it may help to write them up later for their article.

When Jason and Emma woke up the next morning, they heard unusually loud noises coming from downstairs and rushed to check out. They noticed that everyone in the family was quite serious and tense. Emma asked Krish what had happened, and why everybody was so tense.

"It's customary to offer something to the groom, so we planned on giving him 1000 acres of land. However, we discovered today that the land has been inhabited by someone, and we're not sure what action we should take at this time. If we don't offer the land, there's a chance the wedding could be canceled."

"Canceled? What?" Emma and Jason were both stunned after hearing all of this

Jason and Emma remained silent since they were at a loss for words. They noticed that the entire family was unified in their desire to assist the bride's father and find a solution to the problem. Krish decided to go to that location and find out what was going on. The land was in Verso, a little town some 200 miles from their location, with lush greenery full of mountains, valleys, and hills.

While everyone was comforting the entire family, Jason asked Krish if he may accompany him. Krish agreed, and they both started driving to that place. After crossing the city and driving for two hours, they arrived in a village where they planned to stop for lunch., They noticed a group of people gathered by the road, and as they got closer, they found a man lying down dead, and the group conversing. When Krish inquired, he was told that the farmer committed suicide because he couldn't support his family any longer due to drought which has been continuous for three to four-year-long. Krish and Jason were stunned after seeing the dead body with the horrendous story. The desire to feed his family and the immense horrifying drought eventually took his life from his own hands. Jason was perplexed and his heart was pounding fast after seeing some of the darkest realities of the world that he had never seen before in his life.

They later arrived at a restaurant and ordered lunch. The server brought out the hot lunch, which included a variety of bread, soups, cooked veggies, and dessert. Jason grew pretty hungry after seeing the range of dishes available. He was curious about the food offered in India. Krish explained that there are two types of food-loving communities.- one is vegetarian and the other is non-vegetarian. The non-vegetarian community enjoys chicken, whereas vegetarians love plant-based foods.

Krish began to express his sadness about the situation while eating lunch. "This part of the town is facing the worst water crisis and it is hurting especially farmers who are dependent on rain. It's the only bread-earning work they have, and if they are not able to sustain such harsh conditions without help from the government or other organizations, they have no other option except to commit suicide or relocate to the city and acquire a new job that they are unfamiliar with."

"I see that people are facing a disastrous phase of their lives. For the government, it seems preposterous but for the poor fragile people it's a matter of death...." Jason said while controlling his emotions.

"Millions of people are affected by the water crisis, and quite often you hear farmers commit suicide in this country as a result of drought, a risky credit system, crop failure, low wage, no alternative income, and debt," Krish explained the intensity of the situation

"Why is the government not doing anything about the farmer crisis?"

"Yes, the government has a subsidiary and funding program assistance system, but it does not reach farmers on the ground. The money is largely distributed to seed producers, dealers, and corrupt politicians, not to farmers. Also, the funds get distributed to cities rather than small towns and villages where there are farmers..."

"I feel it is a major crisis that must be addressed in order to prevent farmer suicide,"

"Yeah, and for now let's pay the bill and resolve another problem and slouched into the solutions..."

They continued their journey and came to a section with rich greenery of mountains and valleys. A small lake formed below from the waterfall that dripped off the edge of the mountains. While admiring nature, they both got delighted and they both looked serene while enjoying the cold breeze. Later, they arrived in the town where the land was located and were astounded to see that someone had occupied and built a tiny house on the property. Krish said to Jason to stay in the car and that he would go and enquire about it. As Krish approached the gate, a pair of huge men with a large stick used as a weapon approached. Their eyes looked furious while they evaluated him with a frown look.

"Who are you and what do you want?"

"It's my land. Who are you to occupy it and build a house on it?"

"Our boss Mr. Sinha owns this land, therefore if you have any questions, you should go and ask him. He lives 20 minutes away from here in the center of Suki town."

Krish realized that talking to these guys was pointless and he would rather meet their boss and evaluate the whole situation after negotiating with him. Krish came back to the car and they started driving to Suki town.

"How can someone occupy someone's land and claim ownership of it? Don't you guys have legal records and data maintained in the housing department?" Jason asked Krish in detail.

"Yes, we have legal documents registered but people here produce bogus documents with power and money. They re-register and occupy land, this is also one of the major issues, police don't have much say on this since they don't have much power to prosecute and when somebody files a lawsuit, it takes 5-10 years to get a court settlement. This is one of the reasons, most of us like me, make direct contact with the individual and settle down"

"I'm stunned. 5 to 10 years in a court settlement? Dude.... that's a hell of a lot difficult for me to comprehend. Now I know why everyone was so agitated after hearing the news..." Jason said while imagining what happened at Krish's house

"That's the way the world is going on right now, Jason..."

They arrived at Sinha's house, and Krish walked inside to inquire. As he got closer, he spotted a large crowd waiting to meet Sinha, and he discovered that he was also a politician. He waited outside until his turn came to meet him, as he went inside they got stunned after watching him.

An elongated man in his 50s holding a cigar and playing with the smoke. His jawline was round and his hair was immense black with a long mustache. He had a light brown complexion. He seemed a bit arrogant with a tough personality. Krish engaged in a discussion with him while introducing himself, then brought up the subject of unlawful land grabbing and informed him of the seriousness of the situation. The politician was smart, he said that the land belongs to him and Krish had a bogus document.

"A bogus document? Are you kidding me? How is that even possible?" Krish said while being extremely infuriated.

"Everything is possible in this strange world..."

They argued for some time, later politicians gave a proposal for Krish to pay him 20 lakhs (around $25k) and he would hand over the papers and land to him. Krish was a bit confused about the whole situation and he can't get to the final decision without his family's input. Krish told him that after consulting with his family, he will inform him about the proposition.

Krish made a phone call to his dad and told him

everything about the proposal. His father was leaning toward paying the cash because his daughter's wedding was more important than fighting and reclaiming the property, which could take years, but there was one problem: he didn't have the funds to pay right away because the majority of the money had already been spent on the wedding.

All the relatives who were listening to the conversation immediately gathered and chipped him the money. His dad was very happy to see the family unity during these troubled times. He called back Krish and specified that he is transferring the amount to the politician. They were able to settle the sum and reclaim their land. The politician handed over the papers and headed back to his main chamber. Krish and Jason started driving back to their house while resolving the major conflicts, otherwise, the wedding would be jeopardized.

7

"Jason, there is an Ashram on the peak of the mountain. Do you want to see it? It's only a 30-minute detour from our planned itinerary and there's a very wise old master named Satyaji yogi. Do you want to meet him?" Krish asks as they were driving. "I've been there several times; Emma inquired about meeting spiritual gurus in India; nevertheless, since we're here, I can introduce you to one of them," Krish continued.

"Of course, I'd like to meet him, even though I'm not a religious/spiritual person," Jason responded.

"You don't have to be a religious/spiritual person. It's something different that you experience in presence of this master which I like, that's why I come here frequently to see him."

They began driving at the mountain's crest, which was surrounded by dense forest, and the roads were incredibly narrow and zigzagged. Because of the state of the road conditions, they narrowly escaped a collision; there was no side protection during few turns. Finally, they arrived at the top of the mountain, where they discovered a magnificent Ashram tucked away from the bustling town.

As soon as Jason stepped out of the car, he felt the nice breeze and he was enveloped by clouds at the bottom of the hill where he was gazing. The atmosphere was serene and tranquil, with gardens, flowers, and a fountain as they entered the main ashram from the gate. Jason noticed a few monks meditating calmly on the right side. and as they climbed the steps, the wise master came out and greeted them. Jason never expected a master to come out and greet them, usually, people stand in lines for hours together to meet masters, Jason thought.

Jason was enthralled by his appearance; this master was one-of-a-kind, with white hair and a long beard that drew him like a magnet; his face was radiant, and Jason pondered how huge his aura would have been if it had been visible.

Krish introduced Jason to the master, and they conversed almost for an hour while food was served. Finally when they started leaving the master told Jason "You are a good man Jason, your aura reveals it, you just need to channel your energy in the right direction to have a fruitful aim in your life"

Jason nodded his head in front of the master "Thank you, master; my life has been mysterious; I sometimes wonder who am I really and why my life is like this."

Master with a short smile "You will come to know, there is a lot to learn in your Journey."

Jason didn't understand what the master meant, but it was time to leave since Krish had a huge task to fulfill at his sister's wedding. They both said goodbye to the master and headed home.

Back at home, there were numerous events going on, and everyone was relieved that the marriage would proceed as planned and there would be no further obstacles.

Finally, the marriage ceremony has arrived and there is a huge crowd of relatives in the ceremony. Meanwhile, Jason and Emma indulged in assisting the family with all the problems that were being arrived at during the marriage ceremony. Emma dashed inside the bridal room to assess her friend's wedding gown and her own attractiveness in it. When Emma entered the room she saw her friend wrapped in the color red while wearing traditional jewelry. Her hands were full of Mehandi and she was looking stunning in the elongated red saree.

"You are looking gorgeous. I don't know how to explain in words..." Emma said while she had tears in her eyes.

"I'm glad that you came here from the US just to attend my wedding. It means a lot to me. Now I can't wait for when someone steals your heart and I can get to see your big day as well," Both started laughing. Emma brought Myra to the main wedding as the bride's maid. All the traditional customs took place and the groom tied the knot with the love of his life. And the time arrived when Myra had to say goodbye to her family, friends, and everyone connected to her. She was entering a new phase of life while leaving her previous life behind. A new phase of life with different conflicts and everyone was getting emotional. Myra's tears rolled down her cheeks while seeing her parents so gloomy on her Vidai (farewell). Myra's wedding wrapped with her farewell.

8

After the wedding was over Jason and Emma began packing their belongings early in the morning, as they had a late-night flight.

After the hustle and bustle of the wedding, Jason, Emma, Krish, and their parents were watching the news channel early in the morning. Two political parties were arguing about a recent incident. A religious community was rioting in the next neighboring state, and there was a curfew and lockdown. Politicians were yelling and blaming one other's groups for the situation, without any respect for one another.

"Why can't they stay calm and try to do something, find a way to prevent such an incident from happening in the future?" Krish's Dad stated.

"We know that certain political parties may have staged this situation in order to gain sympathetic popularity because the election is approaching, and they need to convey information about their party handling the situation to the general public," Krish commented

"I think it's the same everywhere in the globe, two political parties fighting instead of working together to find a solution," Jason stated.

"Yeah, it's a big issue worldwide, we don't want to scratch our heads on this. Are you both interested in seeing live cricket in a nearby stadium? I bought a couple of tickets for you guys a long time ago when I found out you were coming to Myra's wedding."

"I'm not sure, if we have time to go, we have a flight to catch" Emma answered.

Jason is a sports fanatic, and he immediately responded "We've plenty of time to catch our flight, and it departs at midnight, so we should go check it out."

"Let's get ready, we will leave in 30 minutes."

Later, all three of them left home, heading towards the stadium. It was a one-day international match between India and West Indies. As they reached the stadium, they couldn't believe how packed it was with people dressed in costumes, some of whom had their national flag painted on their faces, chanting, singing the national anthem, and motivating their team. It was very heartwarming for Jason and Emma to watch this, a few hours ago they watched a furious debate on politicians fighting and blaming each other, now suddenly they witness everyone clapping and singing as one.

"There are 29 states in India, with 121 languages

and various religions; the only thing that keeps Indians unified and forgets their differences is national sports like cricket and Bollywood films." Krish spoke loudly in the midst of background crowd noises.

They had a good time and enjoyed the entire game, in which India won by 30 runs. At the conclusion of the game, everyone ran to the center of the stadium with their flags and balloons popping out.

Late in the evening, Jason and Emma freshened before heading to the airport. They had a little talk with the family and Krish. Krish took them to the airport and bid them last goodbye and added "Stay in contact, my friend."

Emma called Myra before heading inside and said her final goodbyes to her.

They boarded and their flight "Eagle Airways, Flight 121" took off, Emma was exhausted and ready to sleep. It was a 17 hour flight; however, Jason was not tired, he told Emma to sleep while he worked on the trip story that would be submitted to Mike for publication. Emma was surprised and noticed Jason was gradually becoming more responsible during this trip.

Jason opened his laptop and began composing his first phrase, "India with 1.3 billion people and great leaders like Gandhi, Subhas Chandra Bose, and Bhagat Singh being born there, encompasses both polarities, like two sides of a coin...," He almost typed for 4 hours and completed drafting the article and emailed Mike for publication. He was weary and exhausted and fell asleep at 4 a.m. Within 30 minutes, everyone heard a loud explosion, and the aircraft was no longer steady. Everyone awoke abruptly, screaming and in panic mode, they saw a gigantic light on the side of their window, the right wing of the jet was on fire. They were all horrified and terrified.

Emma was frantic with worry and she held Jason's hand tightly. Suddenly there was a horrifying movement in the plane and the plane was jerking. The lights began flickering and the engines of the plane were roaring. Everyone in the plane started screaming, as some began having flashbacks of their life. Their memories haunt them due to the immense triggering situation wrapped up with fear.

The flight began jerking, hinting that it would crash at some point. The cabin luggage started falling and smashing the passenger, and the flight was moving downwards with immense speed. As the plane descended under the heavy air pressure, the main door of the aircraft suddenly opened, and the man sitting near the door fell out of the plane while hitting the wings of the plane. Jason and Emma still holding hands, looked into each other's eyes and thought "This is it."

Inside the cockpit, The pilot tried to move the plane upwards but all in vain. So the captain sends a distress signal to ground control in the hopes of receiving assistance. But there were a lot of distortions in the signals and instead lost the signal. Ultimately, After seeing an abandoned airfield, the captain decided to try landing the commercial plane on a shorter runway. They somehow managed to touchdown with one engine, but couldn't control it to reduce the speed. The jet overran the runway and impacted with neighboring shrubs and trees, sparking a large fire and as a result, the smoke engulfed the entire area.

9

Back in the New York office

Mike walked inside the office after grabbing breakfast and a cup of coffee from the outside food truck. On his way to work, he spoke with a few people before turning on his computer and seeing an email from Jason. He read the entire article and became enthralled by the whole story that had been sent from Jason on the behalf of his group, so he quickly contacted his secretary to have it published in the next day's newspaper. Mike sent an email to the entire group informing Jason group story would be published this week and he was astounded and happy after reading their whole story, journey, conflicts, struggle, and how they resolve certain conflicts while using their problem-solving skills.

Meanwhile, Austin checked Mike's response and was so excited and enthralled while seeing the fruitful results of his group efforts and unable to control his emotions.

Meanwhile, Matt slouched in his cube, he was infuriated that his team article was not being published.

"Don't worry Matt. You should have this potential to accept if your competitors won this time..." Austin snarled

"It's preposterous, isn't it? You are happy as if you haven't seen good remarks in your life." Matt frowned and went away while portraying his aggressive attitude.

The time has arrived for the arrival of Jason and Emma. Everyone was waiting for them impatiently as they were on the elongated trip and coming home after a wedding. Their parents were enthralled and were making arrangements at their home for their arrival.

The parents were getting ready to pick them up in the evening. Jason's mother was overjoyed at his homecoming and prepared a delicious lasagna, Jason's favorite dish. On the other hand, Jason's father was communicating with Emma's parents as they decided to go to the airport together to surprise them.

Suddenly, someone rang the doorbell, and it was Austin, who was quite serious and flustered. His heart was pounding fast and he was deeply worried about something. As he spoke with his mother, he rushed to turn on the television and requested both of them to come and sit near it. He kept changing stations until he found a BBC channel where they were discussing a missing plane, Eagle Airways Flight 121. The headline popped up on television:

"With a heavy heart, we are reporting that Eagle Airways Flight 121 had been missing for hours. According to certain sources, the department lost contact with the pilot abruptly, and at first, they considered the weather conditions, but now the situation seems different. The last contact, the flight was in touch with the ground crew somewhere in the Middle East. Will have more details as we come across..."

Parents became afraid and panicked. Austin made a call to Emma's parents and explained the whole situation to them. Everyone was astounded and flustered due to the extremely complex horrifying situation. Jason's mother started crying and she was deeply frantic with worry.

She said to her husband "The worst part of the situation is when you don't know what to do, where to go, and how are you gonna find out details. Everyone will patronize you, but no one will give valuable information about our son."

Meanwhile, Emma's parents reached Jason's house, as Austin called them. They were at a loss and agitated. Jason's dad called his politician friend to see if he had any information about the trip. The politician tried to console him by stating that "The flight is missing somewhere in Syria, which is currently in the midst of a conflict. The governments of various passenger countries are attempting to communicate with Syrian officials on the ground. but due to the war zone, none of the other countries can intervene at this time; therefore, a negotiation is underway. As time goes on, we'll have more information about this. Be calm, Edward. I'll find out more".

Later in the office, Paul and Mike were having a serious discussion about the occurrence, and they were aware that Jason and Emma were on that flight, and that they were on a business trip, so they must act quickly. They contacted a few people they knew to find out what was going on. Every news reporter from around the world was spreading the news that the government is trying its best to make contact with the Syrian government. But due to the war situation, it's getting worse to get more details.

10

Somewhere in Syria.

A few hours after the crash, only a small bit of the last part of the plane is undamaged and has been resting apart a few yards from the rest of the plane. All passengers in the front 3/4th of the plane, including the captain and co-pilot, are dead. Their blood was flowing as their souls departed from their bodies. A few of them, towards the back of the plane, survived. The entire area was in terrible condition, and all of the passengers' belongings were imperiled. Many people were dead, burned in the hellfire. Few of them who survived were unconscious and suffering from injuries. Jason survived the crash but his leg was trapped in a crumbled seat, with blood on his thighs and scratches on his face. He made a valiant effort to escape, and after an hour or so, he emerged out with less leg injury.

As he emerged and began searching for Emma, he

heard a female voice, "Help me, help- anyone..." and as he got closer to the source of the call, he spotted a seriously injured woman and a 7-year-old child. Jason rushed towards them while struggling with his physical pain. He assists them by bringing them out of the plane; the boy survived without injury; however, the lady had small scratches and said that her husband was still inside. When he returned inside to look for him, he discovered that her husband was already dead. Jason couldn't control his emotion, he felt like vomiting and his eyes were in tears. He made himself stop crying and gathered the courage to let the mother of the child know about this horrendous reality.

"Where is my husband? Is he there?"

"I know this is hard for you, but you have to be strong for your son," Jason said while mumbling something.

"What do you mean by this? What happened? Is he alright?"

"I'm so sorry for your loss. He is dead...." the woman screamed and fell down and became unconscious.

Jason suddenly held her up and screamed for help, but there was no one to help. He asked the boy to stay with his mom, while he go out and look for someone. Jason continued looking for Emma, but he couldn't find her inside the plane. When he began to examine his surroundings,, he discovered that all of the plane components were strewn across a mile. He observed an airline seat lying unharmed from afar and noticed a girl's hair blowing in the breeze from behind. He ran toward that direction, with uncertainty, and eagerness, as he got closer and turned around in front of her, he was relieved to find out, it was Emma. He tried shaking her awake, screaming to hear a reply back, but she was still unconscious. He attempted to locate and bring water to splash on her face. She slowly opened her eyes and saw Jason. He had a scratch on his face and tears in his eye. He unbuckles her seatbelt, hugged her tight, and kisses her forehead repeatedly. Except for a few scratches here and there, she had no serious injuries on her body as well. This was the first time he felt pure love, and he realized his life would be meaningless without her. His feelings for her grew enormously. They both gathered their courage and started looking for other survivors and made a spot outside the crashed spot, where they were gathering every survivor.

Sky was covered with smoke and darkness was spreading everywhere. There was a fire in the bushes depicting the chaos in the area. Asif, a young man driving an SUV, spotted black smoke at a distance. He was well aware that his country was a war zone, and that there was always a conflict raging between various isolated fanatics. As he got closer, he noticed something strange. There was no fighting, but rather, smoke with large metal pieces on fire and some entirely burned out. He concluded it was a plane as he got closer. He parked his van on the side of the road right away and dashed towards the crash site. His throat was affected by the immense horrendous smoke but he went there to save any potential survivors.

He noticed that two people were searching for survivors as well. He walked closer, it appeared to be Jason and Emma. He introduced himself as Asif and offered them his assistance and support.

"Where is this place?" Jason asked Asif.

"Outskirts of Damascus, Syria". They were baffled by the fact that they were in Syria.

"What? We are in Syria. In the middle of the war zone..how is this possible?" Emma frowned

"Anything is possible in this strange, horrendous world..." Asif said to Emma while evaluating the whole situation.

"We need to look for survivors, help us." Emma requested.

Jason, Emma, and Asif went to see how Miyung and Saem (the lady and her son) were doing. Jason instructed Emma to remain with them while he and Asif searched for other survivors. The lady was physically, emotionally, and mentally shattered, and she was still dealing with her pain and despair.. Emma approached them and attempted to comfort them. She came to know that Miyung, Saem, and her husband were from East Asia, and they were on their way to the United States via Mumbai on connecting flights.

Jason and Arif were continuing to look for survivors when they came across a man who was hanging on a tree limb and was partially conscious. Asif climbed the tree and attempted to gently pull him down. They offered him water and wiped his face. He returned fully to his conscious state of mind a few minutes later. He introduced himself as Richard, a 58-year-old Atlanta native who worked for a multinational corporation and was returning from a business trip. He was badly hurt, and blood was gushing from his waist. Jason cinched his waist with a piece of cloth. They took him in their arms and began walking towards Emma. As they were heading, they noticed a burned missile hooked to one of the wings as they approached. Finally, they discovered the jet had been shot down by a missile.

"If I'm not mistaken, one of the extremist groups would have shot down while thinking that it was an enemy plane."

"What? Why would the flight path be in a war zone? Usually, if there is a conflict in that nation, the planes are diverted." they were silent, they didn't know the answer.

"There is a lot of mystery behind this incident, is there any secret organization agenda? " Emma commented

"It's merely an assumption. We still don't know anything..." Asif said in return

"It's not safe to stay here since they'll kidnap you and any survivors as hostages and try to bargain for money to finance the war. I strongly encourage you to leave this location immediately."

"You are right. But where shall we go? We don't know any place here..." Jason said to him

"I can take you all to my house in Damascus and then we can work out where you want to go from there. Also, some of you are critically wounded and need to be treated."

"That would be great. Sir, we shall never forget your assistance." Jason remarked to him, placing his hands on his shoulder.

"Don't call me sir, just call me Asif. Hurry up...."

All five survivors sat in the van and they were on their way to Damascus. Jason sat in the front with Asif, Emma, on the other hand, sat in the rear of the van with the other members, and they all proceeded to Asif's house while assessing their surroundings. There were no other survivors, everyone were dead.

11

While Asif was driving them home, the survivors remained mute, and still attempting to figure out their circumstances. A few minutes later Jason made the first move of asking

"Asif, tell me about the situation here,why is there a war?"

Asif started explaining "The civilians raised a conflict against the existing democratic government. The political leader of the Democratic government in Syria, Mr. Emir, declared that they will never hand over their government to the uncoordinated alliance. While on the other side, the civilized party and its alliances aim to rebuild Syria as there is a continuity in the economic and political loss. The leader of the civilized party, Mr. Aftab, declared that they demand a sacred sense of equality among the people of this country. The existing government Initially promised to evacuate the hunger and disparity in society. His party clearly described its intentions toward serving the nation but soon things turned out quite different. The party that claims to bring peace became the worst peace breaker in history. The party became more corrupt and greedy for power, they surreptitiously began removing public funds and depositing them in their personal accounts.

Soon there was a terrible downfall being faced by the country's economy and here comes the rise of the Civilized Party. The proposals diverged dramatically from one table meeting to the next, resulting in a series of lengthy arguments. From here the war behind the political battlefield exceeded its limits. The civilized party declared war against the Democratic Party. The alliance was a win-win game for the civilized party to take over the country. On a safer note, the Democratic Party requested help from the United Nation and NATO powers for help to settle down the situation but no one knows the water has been raised above its level. Many extreme groups developed from this chaos, two such strong groups were FSEG and SPG"

Everyone in the vehicle was paying attention to Asif's words and began asking questions, which he began addressing one by one as they drove toward the city.

The background story behind the plane crash is that SPG misidentified the plane and considered it an enemy plane and launched a surface-to-air missile, which brought the plane down. As the plane was struck, it caught fire and was swiftly dropping; both the extremists and SPG knew this, but they couldn't do anything at the time. And it was all a mistake of their misinterpretations. After a few minutes, they witnessed a massive plane blast, which resulted in a fire and dark clouds. Both groups started heading towards the plane, 20 miles away from the crash but they were in separate locations. Both radicals had the same purpose in mind: they intended to seize control of travelers as hostages in order to demand ransom from their respective countries so that they could fund their civil wars. There was only one road leading to Damascus, and as SPG with 2 trucks and personnel sitting back with guns approached, they noticed an SUV approaching them from the opposite direction.

"What the hell? They are coming. We have to do something about it" Asif groaned while holding his steering wheel tight.

"Emma, hurry up. All of you hide beneath the seats and no one utters a single word.." Jason said to Emma

"Everything will be fine. We have to be strong..." Emma was mumbling while keeping herself calm in this cumbersome situation. As soon as Asif saw the extremist van from afar, he urged everyone to bend fully beneath the seat. The SPG didn't think to stop the car because there was only one guy driving it, and they were in a rush to get to the plane scene. One of the individuals in the second SUV apparently noticed a few people hiding inside, but he didn't think much of it. Later, SPG came to the area and spread out across a

2-mile radius in search of any survivors and valuables. After an hour, they all gathered and came to the conclusion that no one had survived. Later, the person who observed the people hiding in Asif's car instantly informed the leader that he saw a few people hiding inside the van an hour ago. He burst out in anger for telling him late, he recognized them as survivors and he devised an immediate plan of action to locate the vehicle as soon as possible. He dispatched one of his high commands to track them down and apprehend them immediately.

Few minutes later, the second fundamentalist FSEG arrived in the area, and they conducted a similar hunt for survivors and valuables. But again they didn't find anything productive for their hunt. They saw several footsteps and car prints in the area and comprehended the whole situation accordingly. They somehow learned that SPG was attempting to kidnap the surviving passengers, so they followed in their footsteps to kidnap the hostage.

12

As Asif and the group arrived in Damascus, they noticed that most of the city's buildings had been destroyed by the war, and there were only a few people on the road. Smoke was emerging out from everywhere, no street lights were there and most of the roads were blocked.

"What happened to the people?" Jason asked Asif.

"Most of them have left the city and are taking refuge in neighboring countries, or some are still trying to leave the country, only a few of them who are used to living in the city have stayed."

"I can't believe something like this could happen to people in this world. It's so heart-wrenching." Emma frowned

"I was in a similar scenario in my country, so I was ultimately able to secure a visa to migrate to the United States. But now my spouse is dead, and I'm not sure what I'll do there without him." Miyung stated with tears in her eyes.

"There is always light in the world of darkness and I'm sure you will find your own destiny.." Emma consoles Miyung while telling a realistic point of view.

They all reached Asif's home and to be cautious, he parked the car inside his shop. After parking the car he escorted the group inside his home. He introduced them to his wife and two 5-year-old twin girls. His wife welcomed them with a big heart and took all of them towards the lounge. Asif closed all the windows and doors of the house so that no one could see from the outside. Asif's wife got water for all of them and started preparing dinner for them. Meanwhile, some of the passengers started to take a shower and many of them who were injured badly were laying down in the lounge. Emma went into the Kitchen to help Asif's wife so that she wouldn't be burned out due to a lot of hectic activities.

"I need to find a doctor to treat you all. Richard is bleeding profusely, and we can't go to the hospital. I know someone who can assist me in finding a doctor to treat you all." He called his friend's number and spoke to him in Arabic. He was trying to leave the house to bring the doctor to his residence.

Jason stopped him "It would be highly dangerous if you go outside now. As you know extremists are revolving around the streets"

"Don't worry at all. I will keep my profile low and I'm not taking my van for now," he stated while wearing his elongated coat and hat and set out to bring the doctor home.

Meanwhile, Jason was taking care of Richards and looking out for his needs. He observed Emma assisting others despite her suffering and discomfort in an unfamiliar country., His love for Emma was sparkling in his heart. He recognizes the significant role she is playing in his life and feels incredibly grateful of her presence. Their relationship is a testament to the power of love and the importance of having a supportive partner to navigate life's challenges together.

Later Asif and the physicians arrived, the doctors examined each person's condition and prescribed medication, but Richard's health condition was so terrible that the doctor treated him as best he could before stating that Richard needed to be hospitalized or he would die. They need to go to another town to treat him because there is no hospital in the city and everything has been destroyed; however, it was late evening and there is no use in traveling at night. Everyone was worried and flustered about Richard's health but they all couldn't let him down. A few minutes later the doctor left. They all went to bed later that night. After a few hours, a phone started ringing continually past midnight, Asif woke up and picked up the phone. The doctors were on the other end of the line, and he told Asif to leave the house immediately with the guests. The SPG group came to his house to see if there were any foreign guests residing there, as they suspected that they might come to his house for treatment. Two members of the SPG group are stationed outside his house. Asif sprang out from his bed and he slightly saw from the window of his room and he saw two strange men standing outside of his home. SPG and FSEG are searching every residence to find out where they are, and they are hunting for a Black SUV in particular.

Asif rushed towards the lounge to wake everyone up and told them that they need to go right away because extremists are after them. They all approached Asif for assistance because they don't know where to go and are unfamiliar with the culture and language. After some consideration and discussion with his wife, he agreed to assist them. His wife showed resistance at first in helping them because she was afraid of the extremist and she heard horrendous stories about them. Once she heard they used to decapitate people for their own sake and the one who seemed a threat to them. She didn't want to lose the love of her life but Asif being the Asif. He convinced her but she felt bizarre for everything that was happening around her. They all took their belongings, and Asif selected a few items from his house. He kissed his girls while they were fast asleep and bid farewell to his wife.

"Take care of yourself and the girls. I will be back asap." Asif said to his wife.

"Promise me, you will come back. No matter what happens......"

"I will promise you.I will be back, lock the doors

when we are all out of here..." Asif said to his wife while kissing on her forehead.

They began leaving the house in the middle of the night while walking carefully. They walked for about an hour when they heard a truck approaching, and they all ran for cover. SPG members passed by, and they were making loud noises with gunfire in the air. As they leave, Jason and the others continue walking while Asif and Jason hold Richard's left and right arms, respectively. Saem was being held by Emma. After 2 hours or so, they reached a valley, a place to hide. Asif carried a tent and food to eat in his bag. Emma and Jason went there to find some bricks to put on the fire so they can cook some food for survival. They put on the fire and Emma cooked food for everyone. He pitched a tent over there, and they all sat together, exhausted, till 5 a.m. and then went to sleep.

The SPG members arrived at Asif's house early in the morning, knocking hard on the door. Razmi, Asif's wife was terrified, so she checked to see if her girls were sleeping. Her heart was pounding fast and she started crying abruptly. She felt all alone and miserable in this cumbersome situation and she was badly missing the emotional support and back of her husband. She unlocked the door, and as soon as she did, a group of five members rushed in, inspecting every corner of the house. She was tense since she knew the van was parked in a shop downstairs. She evaluated that these members were highly vigilant and they are going to check every corner, every basement of the house. She was getting flustered due to her conflicted emotions and thinking patterns.

"Can I ask you where your husband is right now?" one of the members questioned.

"As I told you before, he is out buying groceries for the home. Men do things for survival and that's exactly what my husband is doing right now," she said in return

"We will highly appreciate it if he is doing exactly what you are saying. Otherwise, everyone has to face consequences of their actions..." he looked at her in a sarcastic way while making his point. They did not find anyone and were leaving, then one of the last members was still in the other room and noticed a door downstairs. He signaled her to come there

"What is this? A door?" His curiosity led him to ask "where it's leading ....".

She became fearful and agitated. "There is nothing over there. It's an empty room...." she answered.

"Unlock the door, right now.." he said with his havoc voice

"As I said, there...." he interrupted her while she was saying something.

"Unlock the door right now...." he yelled at her again, and she proceeded to grab the key, and slowly opened the lock.

"Turn on the light..." he said sternly. It was pitch black inside. When she switched it on, the light flickered for a few seconds before becoming stable. It's the carpet store's back door. He noticed carpets all throughout the place. As he moved deeper into the building, he discovered something wrapped in the shape of a van. He approached and raised his hand to pull the cover, and Razmi struck him with a metal lamp from behind, knocking him unconscious. She hurried out and shut the door. Meanwhile, his group upstairs yelled his name, telling him to come out, and that we should leave now, but there was no reaction or any voice. Ramzi came upstairs and stood next to her girls. They all began looking for him by calling his name but there was no reaction. They assumed he had left and gone out, or that he was in the truck. They started walking out the door when they heard a bang, which they assumed was someone attempting to knock on the door. They all tried to follow the sound, which led to a basement door that Ramzi had shut. They opened it from the outside, and a gang member emerged with blood on his head, telling them that he had discovered the black van they were looking for. They all rush upstairs, slamming into Razmi and aiming guns at her head, demanding to know where her husband is. They struck her again and asked her to tell them about her spouse, but she didn't open her mouth.

"If you don't tell us where your husband is then I'll kill them," one of the members said, pointing a gun at their daughter.

"No, please. Leave my daughters. They are innocent...." She hurried to them and began embracing them tightly, crying. But they didn't listen to her and struck her again.

In the end, she was forced to inform them that they would be traveling to the valley. The group conversed for a few minutes before taking Razmi & kids as hostage.. She hesitated at first, but she had no choice but to obey their commands. She sat behind the vehicle with the gang members, holding both of her children, as they drove towards the valley.

13

The group in the Valley was debating over the conflicted opinions. Everyone was giving their opinion of their next destination and the debate was going on. Abruptly, Jason encountered the idea and suggested traveling toward the neighboring countries on the south side where the border was closer.

Asif added, "It's not safe to proceed south because they'll be on high alert everywhere since they know we're leaving and our next move will be the south border."

"How about the Israel-Lebanon border?" said Emma.

"It would be the same case."

"What do you suggest then?" Jason asked.

"I think we should go north to Turkey. They won't think we would travel such a big journey all the way to the north." Asif said while brainstorming the whole plan of action.

"It's a good idea. We have a child and Richard is hurt, so we shouldn't take any chances." Jason agreed with Emma and Asif, and they all started packing.

As they are packing, they hear the sound of a truck approaching from afar. They quickly recognize that someone is looking for them, and they all rush to the bushes to hide. They got confirmation that it was the SPG group as the truck moved closer and closer. The sound of the truck slowing down can be heard by Jason and the team, and the leader got out of the truck to check, using his binoculars to inspect every position. He noticed two or three people hiding behind the bushes and shouted at them to come out. Jason and his team ignored them; later, he requested that other gang members bring Razmi and the kids out.

"We have your wife and kids and if you don't come out, we will kill them."

Asif began to panic and he didn't know what to do. He started to approach them, but Jason grabbed him.

"What are you doing Asif? We have to plan something else. There should be some other way..." Jason whispered.

"It's all over, we have to get out towards them, or they'll kill them," Asif said and began walking towards them. One by one, the others began rising up and started walking toward them.

Asif approached the commander and leaned down in front of him. The leader kicked him in the legs, and

Ramzi pleaded with them not to hurt him. The leader then walked towards the Jason team, with the gang members pointing guns at them all. The leader made eye contact with each person as he went toward them.

"What were you all thinking, hmm? That you will get away from all of this?"

"You are the devil in disguise and the true representation of the embodiment of evil on the Earth..." Emma frowned

"Oh, you pretty girl. It's the real world wrapped up with darkness and for the sake of survival you should seek support from this darkness..."

"It's pretty much your concern and your opinion and that's merely based on an evil perspective...." Emma groaned

Jason noticed the leader's gun was dangling from his side and signaled Richards with his gaze. Richards recognized his signal and gently nodded his head. When the leader approached Richard, Jason took the gun from him and aimed it at him, requesting that the leader order his gang members to lay down their weapons. When he informed them, they all dropped it. Asif rushed over to hug his wife and the girls. Jason ordered Asif and Emma to get all of the weapons. He also requested that the leader hand over the truck key to them. They took the key and the gun. Jason instructed his squad to sit in the truck. Asif brought Richards, who is still hurt, to the truck. They all sat in the truck and he asked Asif to sit in the driver's seat and drag the leader till he reached the truck. Asif and

Razmi were in the front seat of the truck, while Jason Richard, Emma, Miyung and kids were in the back of the open truck. When they began driving, they released the leader, but the leader had another small gun hidden in his leg and shot Richards in the head. Richards fell from the moving truck, Jason tried to catch him, but he slipped. As he fell, he made eye contact with Jason, as if he was saying goodbye. He then fell down and died.

"Nooooo......" Jason screamed with droplets of tears in his eyes.

He was shocked and wanted to go pick him up, but he couldn't because he was dead and the commander was still firing. They abandoned him and drove quickly forward. Asif noticed Richards collapsing and dying through the mirror, but he was powerless to stop the truck which may endanger children and women. At the back, everyone was sorrowful and still digesting the events that had occurred so quickly.

Meanwhile, SPG gang members contacted another gang to come to pick them up and inform their comrades about the situation. In Parallel, FSEG, who had listened to the radio broadcast, could hear what SPG was saying, and they concluded that the hostage team had escaped, and they discovered their location, and began pursuing Jason's squad. Another challenge awaited them.

14

As they get closer to Homa town, they can still hear fire in various parts of the city, and most of the buildings are destroyed. Asif told Jason that he would drive them all to his uncle's house and they all can spend the rest of the day with them. When they arrived at Uncle's house, Asif went inside first to make sure everything was fine before inviting the rest of the group. After a few moments, he emerged with his uncle and requested that everyone leave the van and enter the house. His uncle requested that one of his nephews will remove the truck so that the extremists are unaware of their location. They all went inside, Jason and Emma realized that there were more uncle's families and relatives inside and they were all enjoying tea together. While Jason and Emma were observing everyone from a corner, Asif and his uncle joined them. Asif introduced his uncle's family, stating that he has a 22-year-old daughter and a wife. His uncle then explained the situation in his town.

He informed them that the majority of the hospitals and schools have been destroyed, with some hospitals remaining intact but without doctors or nurses it was impossible to treat patients. They have all fled the country, some have vanished and no one knows where they are, and approximately 8000 people have died in the town since the war began.

There were crimes, including sexual violence against women, and the prison is overcrowded and in poor condition. We are in hell; our living conditions are dreadful; nonetheless, the only chance we have is to be with our relatives and friends, who are currently residing with us and attempting to cope with the grief they have endured. The majority of the town is deserted, with perhaps 10,000 people on their way to other nations as refugees.

"My heart is gonna burst out after hearing this..." Emma said to them

"You are hearing this only. We have witnessed the bloodshed here and the violence, screams of the people..." uncle responded

"I couldn't get this, how can people be so cruel in this world..." Jason groaned

"These are not the people, boy. They are the fiends in the faces of humans..."

"I wish I could do something about it..." Emma frowned

"Just think about yourself and escape from here asap. It's not safe here for you guys."

"But leaving you all here in the middle of the death zone isn't the solution. Come with us." Emma requested.

"It's our destiny girl. We don't want to move away from our destiny. We would love to die in our homeland..." his uncle said to her while dealing with his emotional conflicts.

After some time, Jason made a phone call to Austin,

"Hey buddy, how are you? this is Jason"

"O my god, dude, thank god," he relieved the stress that he has been feeling for the past one week "is Emma Ok!"

"She is fine and with me"

"Where are you guys now?"

"We're in Syria and have misplaced all of our passports, luggage, and money. I need your help. Inform my parents and Emma's parents that we are okay and also I need a new passport since there is no embassy in this conflict zone."

Austin quickly responded, "I would go to the embassy tomorrow morning and secure a temporary passport for both of you, and then come over there with the passport."

"Due to the current circumstances, you cannot enter Syria. As a result, I am asking that you leave for Antalya, Turkey, and wait there while we arrange to flee Syria via Turkey's northern border. The journey might take 3 to 4 weeks."

They spoke for a few minutes and later Jason and Emma went to bed.

On the fourth day, late in the evening, everyone was having snacks and tea. Jason, Miyung, and Emma were chatting with a few elders about what they were doing- most of them being businessmen. One had a restaurant, another had a jewelry shop, and so on. While the elders were chit-chatting, the kids were playing and running between them. Asif told them to play in a room and not to make too much noise. One of Asif's daughters remarked they were bored of playing alone in that room.

Razmi and Noura stood up "Let's play, I'll come with you."

Saem took his mother's hand and invited her to join as well. She agreed to accompany them.

"I'll join as well". Emma walked near them.

"Oh wow...It's gonna be fun." All the kids got excited.

Asif and Jason were talking to his uncle and other family members, while the women and children entered the room to play.

"Can I borrow your phone?" Jason requested Asif.

"It's in the room, come in, I'll give it to you."

They both went to the same room where children and ladies were playing, and as soon as they arrived, a vibrating heavy sound was heard; it was a missile that had just hit right in the center of the elders' talk. They all stared at one another for a moment and the missile detonated, devastating 3/4 of the home. Everyone was killed on the spot and the room was filled with smoke and fire.

Jason and his friends escaped with minor injuries. Jason checked to see whether Emma and the other kids in the room were wounded, and they weren't. Miyung and Emma began cuddling and comforting the crying children. Asif went to make sure Razmi and the kids were safe. When he and Noura walked outside to check, they discovered that everyone had died.

Noura was looking for her parents when she noticed her mother was dead and her father was badly injured with blood all over him. She and Asif ran to him, removed all the objects that were lying on top of him, and held him. His father took his daughter's hand in his hand and said,

"Asif, take care of Noura, and leave immediately out of this country." he took his last breath and his soul departed from his body.

"No, Abi. You can't leave me here like that. I need you Please come Abi...please...." She hollered as her world was ripped apart within a few minutes.

There were screams everywhere with blood spitting on the floor. In a horrifying scene with blood, everyone can feel the sparks of fear in their body. Everyone was weeping, and Jason's eyes were filled with tears. He was still stunned; he couldn't believe what had happened in just a few seconds. They were all laughing and are now all dead.

But they all have to gather their courage to survive and figure out the next strategy. They started gathering stuff and left with his uncle's van, taking anything they could, with tears in their eyes and headed towards the north of Aleppo.

15

They spent the night and days driving offroad since the main highway was dangerous and they knew SPG and FSEG soldiers would be stationed at checkpoints. Miyung began telling her story as Jason was driving the car.

"I never thought an incident could repeat itself like Deja Vu,"

Emma made direct eye contact. "What do you mean?"

Miyung then related her story while she was living in her hometown.

"I used to be a teacher in my own country, and I taught children as young as 12 years old. Our country's atmosphere is fundamentally different from the rest of the world; we are secluded and have no contact with the outside world; we have no clue how other countries or people live. We don't have an internet connection, so social media sites like Facebook, YouTube, and foreign news are out of the question.

Only the tale and leader would be presented on television. Our school curriculum is dependent on our leader, and our everyday activities are closely watched; there is no free choice, and everyone is obliged to obey strict rules and regulations, which makes no sense.

My husband and a group of members were severely attacked and sentenced to five years in prison after attempting to demonstrate a change one day. Often, I used to visit him in jail to check on him. His condition was bad; he had to perform manual work all day and would provide very little food, which was not even adequate to keep their health, nor did they have the stamina to work the next day. They were beaten often, the inner circumstances of the jail were awful, and he served for five years before being freed.

We decided to leave our country for the sake of our son Saem's future so that he would not have to go through what we did. We made the decision to flee through a neighboring country. We were joined by two additional families as we traveled near the strongly guarded northern border between ours and the neighboring country, with only a lake separating them. We knew crossing the river boundary may end in death, but we had no option but to take the risk. The lake was frozen because it was January, making it simpler to traverse but also dangerous because there were only a few spots where the lake was not solid and chance of falling in frozen water.

We determine that all three families will pass during the night when the guards will not be able to see them. We started walking towards crossing the river around 1 AM, in the dark, with the kids sitting on dad's shoulders. Everyone was holding hands and following the footsteps of the person in front of them as we crossed the lake, and were approximately in the center of it. One of the family members stepped on the loosely compacted Ice, it began to fracture and spread quickly, causing both the husband and wife of the family to fall inside, the guards heard the loud disturbance, My husband and another family member attempted to rescue them, but by the time the spotlight was switched on, they had started firing at us.

My husband ordered us to run with the kids since he and his pals were still trying to pick them up. However, a bullet penetrated both the husband's and wife's chests and killed them both instantly. They began to sink, and my husband was stunned to witness them drown. Another buddy shook my husband and said,

"Let's move, they're dead."

They rushed and crossed the border into the neighboring country while the gunshots were still on.

"We had a few contacts in a new country and requested refuge in the United States and were granted a visa to enter the country. We took a connecting trip to New York via Mumbai".

All women Emma, Razmi, and Noura consoled Miyung for sharing her tragic experience. By then, they arrived in Aleppo, and they needed a place to hide for that day, so they came across a small abandoned airport nearby.

As they started heading toward it, a man inside the airport tower was peering out the window with his binoculars at the incoming vehicle; he peeked inside the van, noticed non-Muslim individuals and children, and immediately recognized them. He was aware that FSEG was looking for them. Asif and Jason were unaware that the local abandoned airport was in the hands of the FSEG gang, so the man called the FSEG group that was pursuing them. He informed them that they had arrived here at the airport.

FSEG was an hour from the airport, so the FSEG commander urged the controller to keep a watch on them until he arrived. SPG, on the other hand, overheard their chat on satellite radio and began driving towards the airport. They didn't know that another struggle and a horrendous hurdle were waiting for them. Meanwhile, Jason and his team began looking for a spot to relax for the night. They discovered a piece of the structure that was still standing and began resting there.

"We are in Aleppo, and if we head one hour west, we will reach the Turkey border, and all our problems will be over; from there. We can go to Hatay, the closest refugee camp in Turkey from here. There are approximately 20,000 refugees living there today, out of a total population of 3.5 million. Asif spoke in a low voice and continued "The border gate is now closed and will reopen in the morning, so we should rest here tonight and leave early morning."

"Thanks a lot for helping us, you sacrificed your own peace for us. We are much obliged for whatever you have done for us...." Jason patted him on the shoulder.

"Peace? My friend, We were not at peace from the day the war hit our country. Many innocent lives were lost in front of us and we are helpless and all our efforts were in vain. I didn't want anyone to lose their lives and that's the reason I gambled into it..." Asif said to him while his eyes were filled with tears and his emotions were fluctuating.

Meanwhile, FSEG arrived at the airport and spoke with the guy in charge of the tower. They intended to go in the morning and capture them because it was night and there was a risk of them escaping due to low visibility. SPG arrived as well, and they were stationed on the opposite side of the tower as FSEG. They had also intended to move in the morning to capture them.

The sun rose from the east, and birds began to chirp; Emma felt the cold morning breeze, and her eyes opened. She awoke with the intention of alerting everyone so that they could begin moving toward the border as soon as possible. Everyone awoke and began to freshen up one by one. In the meantime, Jason and Asif were preparing breakfast. Some people were speaking, while others were in deep grief over the awful death of their loved ones. When they were all set, Aisf went to the vehicle first to keep a few things in the van.

While on the tower, an FSEG individual noticed a truck approaching Jason and his squad from afar, he instantly told his leader that SPG is also approaching them. Immediately the leader and his gang began racing towards their truck and heading in the same direction.

Jason and his team were caught in the middle; they had no idea what was going on and were about to depart.

Both FSEG and SPG groups approached from the opposite direction. They saw each other and realized they were both trying to kidnap Jason's crew, so they started shooting at each other.

Jason and his team were surprised and helpless, they were in the midst, surrounded by bullets and nothing to protect them.

For a while, there were a few bullet wounds, and both groups were badly damaged. Eventually, all SPG members were killed, and only three FSEG members remained, forcing everyone to sit on their trucks as hostages. Asif and Jason began fighting and trying to escape from the leader, they seized hold of one of the members' guns and pointed it at the leader, asking him to leave. The leader ordered the other two members to drop their guns; one of the members did, but the other member ignored the order and instead pointed his rifle at Emma's head, threatening to kill her unless Jason dropped his gun. Jason tried to explain that he had a pistol aimed at the leader, but the gang member saw he couldn't, so he took his chance to adhere to his terms and urge them to drop the gun. Finally, Jason had no choice but to leave the leader and drop the gun. The leader immediately snatched Jason's revolver and ordered his gang members to accompany Emma to the truck. They all sat in the truck still pointing a gun at Emma's head,

"If you come any closer, we will kill her,"

Jason and Asif had stood there with their hands up, watching them go with Emma. As soon as they departed, they both sprang inside the vehicle, requesting Miyung, Noura, and Razmi to stay there, as they began pursuing the leader's truck. The leader contacted the tower man and ordered that the plane be kept ready on the runway, and the gang started heading towards the runway. Jason and Asif were far behind the gang and were desperately trying to catch up. The leader arrived near the plane that was about to take off, they dragged Emma inside the plane and immediately began preparing for take off.

As the plane started moving for take off, Jason and Asif began chasing the jet, the boss ordered one of the gang members to open fire on them. He began shooting, but Jason was adamant about stopping the plane; he couldn't picture life without Emma. They knew the plane would be up in the air at any moment, so Asif told Jason to press the accelerator faster. They got almost to the plane's tires, but the plane lifted to take off right away. One of the gang members at the doorway, who was carrying a rifle in one hand and holding an aircraft in the other hand, lost control and fell down. The jet took off without him, and only Emma, the leader, and one other gang member were on board. Jason and Asif came to a halt in the center of the runway. Jason got out of the van, watching hopelessly, and his failure to rescue Emma.

"Emma,......" he whispered desperately

Asif felt his pain and rushed towards him to console him.

"My friend, listen to me. Listen to me. We will find her and she will be with us...." Asif was consoling him but he knew he can't do anything for now to ease his pain.

Later, they went near the seriously injured gang member who was still laying on the runway. Asif grabbed the gun that was lying and pointed at the injured person's head. When Jason inquired as to where they had taken her, the gang member hesitated to respond,

Asif stated, "I'm going to kill you, I'll count three, two...."

"Africa,"

Jason grabbed his collar "where in Africa?"

"Somalia."

Jason's heart was still pounding and craving for Emma, he never felt like this before in his life, losing his beloved, and knowing that he could not do anything. He couldn't figure out why they were taking Emma to Somalia or what was going on. His mind was all over as he imagined awful things happening to her and yelled.

"Please come back to me, Emma."

Asif knew that he cannot do anything to help him, they had no passports and there were no flights yet.

"There is only one way to get Emma. We should go to Turkey and figure it out there. We really need to get out of here my friend"

He consoled Jason and asked him to get into the van, they drove to the location where others and Razmi were halted.

16

After they reached there, they told everyone about the incident. Everyone was shocked; no one ever imagined it could have happened. The women present there were looking at Jason and felt sorry for him. Meanwhile, they drove the van to the border and ditched it 5 miles away from the border, and began walking. Thousands of people were strolling down the road, hoping to cross the border. The situation was chaotic; citizens were fleeing their nation with a little clue where they would find shelter or food in another country.

They arrived at the Turkish border after walking for an hour. The border was packed with people, with camps scattered around, and the majority of them were discussing the situation. Jason and his gang attempted to cross the border, but the gates were closed and many migrants had already been housed in

Turkey. Now the political leaders will decide the future of these people.

They also started setting up their camp to spend the night. Jason could not find a moment where he would not think of Emma. He had kept his emotions at bay, but his thoughts and heart were still on Emma. He could not sleep the whole night, he was worried about his love Emma. He tried closing his eyes, but he would find her in his dream, and anxiety would wake him to reality. The following day Jason got up with puffy eyes, and with a heavy voice, called his dad to explain the situation. His dad promised to try his best to make sure that Jason and his crew members get inside Turkey. After a few hours, Asif's phone rang- it was Jason's father.

"Go to the guard and ask him to let you talk to the captain. They will let you and your friends get safe, do not waste time, just go now."

"Thanks, dad, I'm leaving now."

They rushed to the entrance, but the soldier only allowed Jason through. He stepped inside, waiting for the captain. It took him over two hours to reach out to him. Jason knew that if the team didn't enter Turkey today, he'd never see them again. On the other hand, Asif & his group had lost hope and felt it was fate for them to stay, but Jason returned with some paperwork and passed them over to the soldier, who opened the gates and they all entered Turkey safely.

It was a life-changing moment for Asif and his family, who have been in search of a safe place for so long. They took the bus and headed towards Hattey, which was the first refugee camp. It was quite emotional for Asif and for his family. They bowed down on the ground as soon as they entered the lands of Turkey. Their heads were pounding with different emotions. They were happy for finding a safe spot, but they were also feeling pain for leaving behind everything, their families and friends, yet they were thankful to God and Jason for it.

Jason contacted Austin "It's me, have you reached Antalya, Turkey".

"Yes dude, it's been two days since I've been here, I've your and Emma's passport."

"Alright, I would take the night bus and would meet you in the morning..

"Ok buddy, See you in the morning."

Jason went inside his camp and tried to rest for a few hours. He shut his eyes and went to sleep promising himself that he would find Emma.

Miyung, Saem, and Jason said goodbye to Asif and his family. They hugged each other.

"Can I come with you and help you to find Emma, my friend?"

"No, you need to be here, to take care of your family in this new country. If our destiny crosses again, we will meet," Jason said with heavy hearts and set off to Antalya.

Jason kept thinking about Emma on the bus and tried to focus on locating her rather than weeping in agony. They reached Antalya, Austin was waiting for them, and as soon as they saw each other, they couldn't control their emotions. With heavy sadness, they made the same gesture that they used to do and hugged each other. He introduced Miyung and Saem to him.

"Where is Emma?"

Austin was unaware of the events. Jason narrated the entire story, which left him speechless.

They had lunch in a hotel nearby. Jason told Miyung and Saem a final goodbye,

"Once all of this is sorted out, I'll see you both in the United States."

"Don't worry about us; try to find Emma and bring her back."

And they departed to the US embassy to get their passports and visa to travel back to the US while Austin and Jason planned to fly to Somalia to find Emma.

Austin requested Jason to write everything down and email it to Mike for publishing so that someone may step forward to aid them. Jason felt uncomfortable at first, but he sat down, typed everything down, and mailed it to Mike in the hopes of obtaining some assistance.

Mogadishu, Somalia

They boarded their planes bound for Somalia. It was an eight-hour journey, and Austin fell asleep as soon as the plane took off; Jason couldn't sleep since his thoughts kept him awake. He couldn't fathom himself without her because he was madly in love with her. He kept thinking about the good moments they had together. To him, the days were short but lovely. He was also concerned about how he would find Emma in the most dangerous and violent nation he had ever heard of, especially since he knew no one there. He determined that the first thing he would do when he arrived was research the FSEG leader Abuddin and all of his links in Somalia, as it was the only clue he had to find Emma.

They arrived in Mogadishu, Somalia, and finished the immigration process. After that, they took a cab to the hotel. They had the impression that a car had been following them since their arrival. They arrived at the hotel. Austin was concerned and stated,

"Dude, keep in mind that this is a dangerous place. We must use extreme caution in this situation. We'd never know if someone was planning to abduct us. We shouldn't make any sensible moves without first thinking."

Jason nodded, and they entered their rooms on the hotel's tenth floor. Through their window, they observed a man sitting outside the hotel. They sat silently and began making arrangements to find Emma. They both went out for dinner late at night to a restaurant, and on their way back to the hotel, they observed a man following them.

17

They immediately began running to get away from him, but he began chasing them as well. They both ran around a few street corners to get away from him, but the man did not back off. When the stranger got closer, Jason and Austin agreed to confront him, so they stopped running. Austin found a metal rod, which he carried in his hand, and they started attacking the stranger.

"Wait, wait, don't attack me, I'm not your enemy, I came to ask you something," the man yelled.

Jason and Austin were confused and looked at each other, they let him go, and he stood up and said,

"Look, I am here to help you. I do not mean any harm."

He took out a piece of paper from his pocket, it was Jason & Emma's story of the incident that had happened in Syria, apparently, the story had been published and now everyone knows about it.

"I came here to see if you needed any assistance; I'm willing to help you guys and pay me whatever you can"

They both stared at each other, and neither of them trusted this man.

How can we trust you? We don't even know who you are, and you may be attempting to abduct us. " Jason responded.

"Look, my name is Dalamar, I'm a family man." He took out his wallet. " Here is my Id and here is my family with my mom and 2 sisters."

Jason and Austin chatted for a few minutes before agreeing and offering him $10,000. The man promised to assist them in finding Emma; he agreed to pick them up the next morning and they would all head out to find Emma. Jason questioned him a few details as they walked together.

New York

It is chaotic now in the US as news becomes international. Everyone on television was discussing the sudden kidnap of Emma, it became the headline of the day. People were sharing an article titled *"The Young Journalist got kidnapped in Syria"*. Both parents were worried. Emma's parents were making calls with certain people, they were trying to get in touch with anyone from the government who could help them to find Emma. They knew if they did not do anything, then they would lose their daughter forever. It's a do-or-die condition.

They were making calls and waiting for a miracle

to happen. The pressure on government officials increased as the news traveled around the globe. News channels and TV shows were discussing the incident in Syria, everyone was focusing on how to find her. Jason's parents were worried for him, as they knew that he is not going to return until he finds Emma. He had put himself in danger as well, the situation could be worse, and no one knew if Jason and Austin would return.

Emma's mother was sitting in front of the television waiting for updates,

"Be strong, our daughter was not afraid of them, she did what she could do with bravery. We are her proud parents and we will do everything to find her.

He hugged her "Everyone is talking about it, therefore this is the right moment to put pressure on the authorities and find her. So I'm going to call everyone I know and ask them to join me in protesting and pressuring the authorities to find her."

Emma's mother looked at her husband and nodded her head,

"I hope we find her. I do not want to imagine anything happening to my daughter. Jesus, pls protect her and keep her safe." She cried with tears while holding her hands together and praying.

The next day Emma's friends and family, Jason's family, colleagues, and many others came out together and protested together in front of the city town center. People were chanting and holding different signs that showed.

"We want Emma. Take care of your Citizens, America." The protest was being aired live on television and Officials were discussing it as a national problem. Everyone was putting their effort to find Emma.

"Bring our American citizens back." The powerful loud voice could be heard across the city.

18

Mogadishu, Somalia

The next day, early in the morning someone was knocking on the door of the hotel room. Austin and Jason were getting ready, they looked at each other wondering who it would be when Jason opened the door, it was Dalmar.

"Hello," he said abruptly as he came inside the room.

"Here's a picture of Abuddin, the man who kidnapped Emma." Jason handed the picture to him

Dalmar stared at the photo and said "I know a person who can give us some information about Abuddin. I can take you over there. Hurry up and get ready,"

Austin was ready and offered Dalmar some coffee. Jason dressed up, and they all walked out of the hotel and got into the car.

"How far does he live?" Austin asked

"It's only a 40-minute drive from here. He lives outskirts of Mogadishu"

"Can you tell me anything about this guy?" Jason asked

"He has a lot of information about criminals and terrorists. He used to work for a local newspaper but is now retired. He may be able to provide some information."

Dalmar drove them for 30 minutes to one of the poorest areas, where there were piles of garbage everywhere on the roads, pretending to be a mountain, some of the kids were playing, and some women and children were searching for treasure inside the garbage pile. Austin gave Jason a glance as he observed outside conditions. Dalmar noticed the mirror and said

"This is one of the poorest areas, and the majority of the residents make a living by collecting items from the garbage that can be sold. It's a large dumpster area for the city, but people still live here because they can't afford to live anywhere else."

"I'm not sure why this guy would live here," Austin asked

"He also does not have any money."

They were a mile away from his house when they realized there were no more roads and they had to walk on a pathway leading to his house. They all got out of the car and began walking towards his small homeless shelter, which he had built. While walking, they noticed piles of garbage everywhere, and at a distance, they noticed a small pond, and the water was very muddy and unfit to drink, but people who lived there had no choice but to use it.

"Water is one of the most scarce resources in this area; most of the time, it is a drought, and people fight for water. So they have no choice but to drink whatever is available, even after knowing that it is harmful to their bodies."

"At the very least, they should use a filter before drinking," Austin stated

"This isn't the United States. It's Africa; even if they only get one proper meal a day, that's enough for them. That's the mentality of everyone over here."

When they arrived at his tent, there was no door, so Dalmar lifted the blanket that was acting as a door and called Farez, who was lying in one corner and he shouted,

"Who is it?"

"It's me Dalmar, and I've brought some visitors who are looking for information."

"Get out of here, I don't have any information. I don't know anything."

"Come on, Farez, they've traveled a long distance in search of his girlfriend. Please assist them."

"I don't care who they are or where they have come from. Just go away."

Jason immediately rushed inside and said,

"Look, sir, we could really use your help. My girlfriend has been kidnapped, and if I don't find her soon, they might kill her."

Farez remained motionless for a brief moment, his

gaze fixed on the photograph. Dalmar made eye contact with Jason and whispered about money. Jason understood and nodded.

Dalmar said, "Farez, they're willing to pay you some money."

He stood up and smirked, "you should have begun with that!"

Jason showed him the picture of Abuddin they were looking for.

"I know him, I've written many articles on this extremist. He doesn't stay in one place, he travels across many countries to keep his team together and arrange to fund for the war activities they are involved in," Farez said immediately.

Jason felt relieved that this person knew something, and that it was worthwhile to travel to his location.

"My girlfriend was kidnapped in Syria and brought here on a flight by this man," Jason explained,

"Do you know anything about it?" Austin asked further.

"I don't know about the kidnapping, but if he did kidnap her and took her on a flight to this country, he wouldn't land in Mogadishu, because he has enemies all over here. So instead, he would probably land in a small airport Lambar, which is 2 hours from here. It's a remote location with hardly any planes, but there might be one person working who can give more details about Abuddin and the plane."

"Thank you so much for your help," Jason said,

handing over $300. They left that place to travel to Lambar. Austin started taking a nap in the car while Dalmar was driving, Jason asked

"Have you been to this airport?"

"No."

"I'm not sure if it is safe to go in. We should be careful". Jason was thinking about the previous incident that happened in the airport."

"I think it should be safer since it is a small airport, and as Farez said, there may be only 1 person who takes care of the airport."

Jason relaxed, and they arrived at the airport after 20 minutes. It was a remote desert with a clay sand runway having a small building at the center. As the car was reaching the building, dust was blasting out behind the car making it invisible to see anything behind. They stopped the car and were very careful when all 3 of them were approaching the entrance. There was a man with a table and a book, the walls were ripped, and dirt was everywhere.

"What can I do for you?" said the man sternly.

"We have come to inquire about a plane that landed last week," Dalmar said to him

"You mean, Cessna citation jet."

"Yes, It was a Cessna white color jet" Jason answered

"It landed last week with 3 people and a pilot."

"Was there any white lady in that group?"

"Yes. I witnessed a white lady being held hostage by two men."

"Do you know where they went?"

"They came inside and were waiting for their truck to arrive, they were very rude to her. During one of their conversation, I heard them talking about Sarcade place"

"I know that place. It's one of the violent places, people are distressed because of all the crime, robbery, and killing taking place in that village. Most are trying to seek refuge elsewhere." Dalmar said

"We should leave now," Jason mumbled enough for everyone to hear.

"The village is right in the middle of the jungle, and I don't think they will be staying in the village. We may have to go inside the jungle. We can travel a certain distance in the car, but later we have to hike in order to reach there."

"It doesn't matter where it is. We have to go and get Emma out"

"Let's get all the stuff necessary for us to go inside the forest," Austin stated

"There is a small town called Merca where we can get all our needs and from there we can go to the village."

"Ok, let's go." Jason gave $100 to the man.

"You can come anytime here, sir- if you need any help. I'm always here," he said warmly, happy to receive some extra money.

They all started driving to Merca. After 5 hours of driving, they reached Merca. It was late evening, so they went to a restaurant to have dinner.

"We should rent a hotel for tonight here and go tomorrow morning to the village, it's 2 hours drive from here," Dalmar said

"Yes Dude, I think so, it wouldn't be safe to go in the night to the village." Austin Added.

"Sure, anyway we need to pick up some stuff for our journey inside the forest and the store would have been closed now," Jason said

They ordered their dinner and while waiting for the dinner to arrive,

"Dalmar, you never spoke about yourself. Tell me what you do in general and your family" Jason asked him

"I came from a poor family. I have 2 sisters and a mom, my dad died a few years back. He was killed during one of the riots, so since then I've become the bread earner for the family. I did my education in civil engineering and used to work for a small company in Mogadishu. But since the war began, most of them left the place and nobody was constructing any new buildings or roads. So, the company was closed and I became jobless. It was very hard to get a job after that, so I started finding opportunities on day to day basis for a job and live"

"What happened to your dad in the riot?" Austin enquired.

"He was an iron smith. He made all the kitchen cutleries and knives of various sizes and had a shop in the city. On that day, as usual, he went to his shop in the morning and we knew there was some dispute going on among various leaders of the country about how to run a nation, each leader had their own agenda in mind. It didn't work out and a civil war broke out on that day, there were fights on the street from various groups clashing with each other. Since my dad was an ironsmith, some group came to our shop to take all the knives, but my dad refused to give them. They killed him and took everything and destroyed the shop."

"I'm sad to hear about your father. I don't understand why humans are so desperate for power. There is no value to human life."

"I'm fine now and have accepted life as it is; we've been living like this forever here, constantly with some threat to our lives and living in terror, we've become accustomed to it now."

The waiter brought the dinner, and they all started having their dinner. Everyone was silent and there were no words in their mouth for some time. Later they went to a hotel and checked in, they were so tired that, immediately Dalmar and Austin crashed into the bed.

Jason leaned on his bed and started thinking about Emma and how she would be surviving in this unknown place. After an hour or so, he was in a deep sleep.

19

The next morning, they checked out and started driving.

"Let's go the store to pick some items required," Dalmar said

They went to a store and picked up a bag, filled with food, water, medicine, rope, bug spray, a tent, torchlight, and batteries.

"I guess we are done here with all the items needed, let's head to the village," Jason said.

"No, we still need to go to one more store," Dalmar responded.

"What do we need?"

"We need some Guns."

Both Jason and Austin's eyes widened.

"Why do we need guns?"

"Without it, we'll be in extremely dangerous situations, with no support if things go out of control."

"We never held a gun, so would it make a difference?" Austin asked in trepidation

"Yeah, I'm not sure if we really need guns. We never shot anyone, and I'm also against the use of guns. It brings more harm than safety." Jason said.

"But we are going to a place where it is the most accessible and heavily used in public. It is important to have one, just in case, it is our only resort.." Dalmar said sternly.

"Isn't there anything else that we can use, other than guns?" Jason asked

"We should use a needle weapon, which when released will poke at the enemy and make them unconscious for a while, this is famous in Africa. I've seen it in movies." Austin excitedly stated

"Yeah, he means Tranquilizer pistol, something like that Dalmar."

"All right, let's go to that store and see if we can find something similar."

They all went to the weapon stores and asked the store manager what they were looking for. The store manager was surprised for a moment and later showed them different types of weapons that can be used to make the enemy unconscious instead of using bullets and a gun. They finally brought all the weapons they needed and left for the Sarcade village.

While traveling to Sarcade, Jason recalled a journey he had with Krish in India, where the outer landscape was similar, with valleys and deep forests and a small road, but this time it was the Africa continent. After a few hours, they reached the village but couldn't believe what they saw.

There were army guards everywhere and a tent with many doctors and nurses serving the locals who had been badly injured. As they were entering inside, the guard asked them to stop the car and he started checking the car in and out, they were wondering what this was all about.

"Who are you guys and why are you here?" the guard asked them.

"We have come in search of a girl Emma who we think might have been here" Jason replied.

"Who is she?"

"She is my girlfriend and she has been kidnapped. Do you know anything about it?"

"No sir, you may have to ask someone inside. You can go now." The guard gestured to the location.

"Thank you."

When the guard turned around and departed, they spotted the "UN" logo on their back. They understood it was the UN guarding the village here. They went inside and parked the car on the side of one of the camps. They didn't know whom to contact, there were so many people both villagers and volunteers. They asked a few villagers by showing the photo of Emma and Abuddin but didn't get any details. Later, Jason noticed a young lady doctor attentively helping injured individuals. He went closer to her and said

"Hi.."

While she was still treating the patient, she was

very surprised to hear a voice behind her back that she didn't recognize.

"Hello..." she said, "surprised to meet with a gentleman with no injuries."

"Hi, I'm Jason. How are you doing?" He begins, raising his hand to shake her.

"I'm Dr. Kate" and shook her hands with him.

"What happened here?"

"A few days ago, a very frightening thing occurred in this community. This community was entered by a bunch of fanatics. They confiscated all of their property, food, and farm animals, and threatened some of the men with kidnapping and burning their homes if they did not join their force. Some locals attempted to protect themselves. They were severely assaulted, and some were forced to give up all of their goods, while those who attempted to defend their home were entirely burned to ashes. It has happened quite often, and eventually, it reached human rights activists, and the UN and WHO must intervene to aid them, which is why we are all here." Kate explained.

Jason was silent for a few minutes hearing their story. He looked around and said

"I don't know what to say. I feel very sorry for them. I wish I could help them anyway I can."

"There are ways to help them out. It's just that we have to make up our minds and the path will be shown."

"Yes, I completely agree."

"By the way, why are you here?"

"I came here desperately looking for my girlfriend, who had been abducted by FSEG chief Abuddin. I got a tip that she could be here, but after asking around, no one appears to know anything."

"Do you have a photograph of her?" Kate asked, feeling sorry for Jason.

"Yes. Here it is. " He showed Emma's and also Abuddin's image.

"I know someone in this village, who I think might know something about it. Give me a few minutes. Let me finish treating these people and I can take you there."

"Sure, take your time."

As he was waiting, Austin and Dalmar entered the scene where Jason was. Jason told them that Kate might know someone who might assist us. Austin and Dalmar nodded as they said hello to Kate, who was treating the patient. She said hello slowly.

As they all were waiting patiently, Jason was observing Kate as she patiently, with complete commitment and hospitality, treated the patients with her pleasant soothing words, letting them forget the event that had occurred and putting some brightness into their lives.

After treating all of the patients in the tent for a few minutes. She walked out and greeted Austin and Dalmar.

"Hope this person knows something about it," Jason said

"I hope so too. I treated this man a day back, and a

few villagers were talking about him. Not sure what it was. They were keeping him at a distance, not sure why...." Kate rambled on.

They entered the tent where this man was, they noticed this man was lying on his bed with all bandages tied to his hands and legs.

Kate introduced them to this man through gestures since he doesn't understand English. He nodded his head when immediately Dalmar jumped in and asked this man in his language, Somalia. The man responded to Dalmar and they spoke for quite a while. Dalmar was asking all the questions and was also showing him the photo of Emma and Abuddin.

"This man is from that extremist group. He was forcefully taken 5 years back and has been with them since then doing all sorts of illegal activities, kidnapping, killing, etc. Recently he had a realization that all that they were doing was wrong and when opposed, they beat him to death, so he escaped from them and now he is here in this village" Dalmar told them about his story

"What did he say about Emma?" Jason asked

"Yes, he had seen Emma and other men and women captivated in a cage. They were mistreating them and asking them to obey their orders, otherwise, they would be killed."

"How is Emma Doing?" Jason asked fearfully.

Dalmar asked the man in his language and the man responded.

"Emma is doing fine at the moment. She has been

held with extra security along with another girl since they knew that they would earn a jackpot by trading and negotiating with officials for releasing them."

Jason and Austin got some hope. Jason thanked God for keeping Emma alive.

"Can you ask the man where we can find her?" Austin inquired

After a few minutes of conversing with the man,

"It's in the middle of the forest. They have a camp there with around 50 men defending it. You can get there through a small dirt road, but everywhere along the road, there are his men, always watching, so the best way is to walk through the forest. It takes two to three days, but none of his soldiers will be able to notice if we go through the forest."

Jason and Austin started discussing what we should do. Kate and Dalmar also pitched in and said it would be safer to go through the forest by walking rather than being caught on the road.

Jason agreed and asked Dalmar, "Can you take all the directions needed to go there by this man?"

"Yes, of course" he sat next to the man and started noting down all the information needed.

While Austin asked Jason, "Should we leave now?"

"It's already late, there is no point going today at this hour. I think you should leave early morning tomorrow" Kate said to them.

Jason and Austin looked at each other and thought for a moment. Kate again interrupted as said,

"There is an empty camp with beds next to my

camp. You can stay there for tonight and leave early tomorrow morning."

Jason was pleased " Thank you for your hospitality and for helping us.."

Meanwhile, Dalmar jotted down all of the details. They exited the tent, and Kate escorted them to the rest camp and told

"Freshen up and relax, there will be dinner in a few hours. I will join you guys at that time. I have a few patients to treat" and left.

20

They all came together a few hours later. There were meals lined out on a table, and everyone began taking up a plate and filling it with food before sitting on the ground around the campfire. Austin was seated next to a child and performing magic tricks for him, while Dalmar was conversing with one of the residents over there in their native language.

While sitting next to Kate, Jason said, "how long are you going to be here at the camp?"

"As long as they want me here but as I see. I don't think we will be here for more than a week"

"Why? There are still people who are in serious condition and may require more days to recover."

"I understand, but it all depends on our WHO organization's leadership. Each project that we undertake globally has a budget, and we must adhere to that budget. It all depends on how much finance we have, and we don't have much left, so we may have to wrap up next week, I believe."

"What are these people going to do once you all leave?"

"Most of them will start moving from here since there is nothing left, the houses are burnt, fear of extremists coming back and torturing them."

Jason was thinking in his mind why he was seeing the same type of situation everywhere. Is there something that he needs to learn or understand about life? He had no idea Kate changed the topic and asked,

"What is your story, how did you meet Emma?"

"We both work for the same company. She was my colleague and I was attracted the 1st day I saw her, there is something in her that brings that joy and love within me. I feel that without her, my existence is pointless and worthless."

"You're deeply in love with her," she said as she caressed his hands.

"Yes, that is why I'm so desperate to find her by any means I can, even If it takes my life."

"Don't worry, you will find her without any problems. My instinct tells you will meet her soon."

"I hope so," Jason responded.

They chatted for about an hour before retiring to their tent to sleep. Kate walked to her tent, and the three of them went to their tent. While they were laying on the bed, Austin was doing all sorts of hand gestures to keep the flies away. He couldn't sleep and kept mumbling.

"Dalmar, how do you sleep so calmly?"

"I'm used to it, mosquitos won't bother me."

"I can't sleep here...."

Dalmar got up and went outside, where he collected some leaves, crushed them, and said,

"Put this on your hands and legs, the mosquito won't come near you."

Austin made an awkward face and hesitated to put it on but he didn't have any choice but to put it on. After rubbing his hand and legs, he went to bed, and after few minutes again

"Dalmar. Listen...."

Dalmar was half asleep and said

"Yes"

"Whatever you give me, it is working. I don't feel mosquitoes biting me anymore"

"Good then..." Dalmar responded in a slow tune.

"Go to sleep Austin, you are disturbing, everyone. We have a big day tomorrow" Jason frowned

Austin tried to lift his short blanket, turned his body to the right, and went asleep. The entire camp was lit with small lights and there was silence everywhere except for the guards taking a walk to guard a certain perimeter of the camp.

The next day early morning, Jason woke up from bed and came out with a water bottle. He saw Kate was jogging within the camp, and as he started splashing water on his face, Kate passed by jogging and said

"Good Morning, Had a good sleep?"

"Yes, but not sure about Austin. He was murmuring

in the night" Jason responded. Kate pushed the camp screen door and watched Austin still sleeping, but Dalmar was not in the bed.

"Where is Dalmar," she asked.

"I don't know, maybe he would have gone to the restroom I think"

He came inside the tent and woke up Austin

"Austin, wake up, we should start packing up"

"Give me 10 minutes," Austin murmured while his eyes were still closed.

Dalmar entered the tent, completely freshened up and ready to leave.

"You are all set" Kate stated to Dalmar

"Yes"

"Ok, let me get ready "Jason left for the restroom.

Kate went to her camp as well. After an hour, they all were set, completely packed, and ready to leave.

"Have breakfast and take some food for the journey."

"Of course, thank you for the offering. We need some food, I don't know how I am going to survive in the forest." Austin responded with a weird look to Jason.

"We will be fine, don't worry"

"You have been in boys scouts so you know how to survive but I've never been to any wood in my life."

"I'm there for you to take care of," Dalmar replied.

"You bet you are" he knew Dalmar was local so he would be familiar with culture and survival over here.

They all went to have breakfast. Dalmar and Austin

were sitting at a table and eating while Jason and Kate were standing on a side, holding their plate and eating.

"This is our final goodbye to you, Kate. Hope our paths cross each other again."

"Yeah, but don't worry. You will find Emma, keep in contact and let me know once you find her. "If I'm gone from this place, then take this" she handed over a piece of paper with her number in it.

"This is my number to reach, I'll be heading home in London."

"Sure, I'll be in touch with you."

They all finished their breakfast, lift their bags on their shoulder and all three of them said

"Bye Kate…"

They all started walking on the narrow path inside the forest. She watched until she could see them and as they entered inside the forest, they were no more. She felt she had some connection with them and finally she was left behind to treat the patients. She wanted to go with them and help the love birds to find each other but due to her presence needed here, she was stuck. Her own love was full of emotional conflicts and she lost someone in her own life. So whenever she sees someone dealing with these emotional conflicts, she desperately wants to help them..

21

The forest is surrounded by a lush environment and many species live within it. The world inside the forest is vastly different from the world outside. Nature is unique, and the wind is warning of something strange that seems bizarre. Early in the morning, it was sunny, but when they reached the dense woodland, they couldn't see the sun anymore. The sky had been covered by long, wet branches and clusters of leaves that concealed the sun's beams. Each tree was massive, with roots sprouting everywhere. Various colored leaves were strewn about as if a red carpet had been laid down on which no one had ever walked before. They couldn't hear any man-made sounds other than birds singing in synchronization as if the forest were hosting an orchestra.

Dalmar was leading them, holding a map that he had drawn while Austin and Jason were following him.

Jason was so mesmerized by his surroundings, he forgot why he was there. It was such a pleasant impact that he was having at that moment, and there were no words uttered by anyone for quite some time. Everyone was in that same vibration, resonating with each other and enjoying nature. They had been walking for quite some time when Austin said,

"Are we there yet?"

"Are you kidding man? It takes 3 days..... we didn't even complete a day" Dalmar answered

"You are acting like a child...." Jason responded.

"Are we there now....?" Austin asked again.

"Not yet....." Dalmar responded.

"I know but I'm tired. We need to take some rest. We have been walking for 5 hours" Austin complained, already stopping to find a clear space where he could rest for a while.

"All right, let's take a break. Dalmar?" Jason stated.

Dalmar looked at the map while evaluating the area they still have to cover. "Ok, there is a place where we can take a rest a couple of minutes ahead."

"Why can't we take a rest here?" Austin said, pointing at a small clear area.

"We need some water. Can you hear the sound of water?" Dalmar responded.

There was silence for a moment and everyone could hear the sound of water falling at a great distance.

"I think I hear a small stream just down that direction," Jason said

"Fine..... I guess I can walk for another 30 minutes," Austin frowned, kicking a small rock in front of him.

They all walked in that direction until the sound of water became louder and they could see a small waterfall and a stream.

"Finally! I'm not getting up once I sit." Austin said happily, as he sat on the hard ground and dipped his feet into the stream.

Dalmar laughed in response as he joined Austin.

"Alright, let's have a break here. Let's have some food and then we can leave," Jason also joined them.

They took out their bags to find the food they had brought. As they were eating, Austin became aware of a noise emanating from above. When he looked up, he saw a monkey sitting on a limb, observing them. As Austin was staring at the monkey, the monkey snarled. Austin decided to make a similar face, mocking him. After some time, Austin gave up and instead, opened his bag and took out a banana. He started raising his hand to give it to the monkey. The monkey calmed down immediately and hesitated to walk down initially but was also eager to take the banana. He slowly came down and stood in front of Austin. He grabbed the banana from his hand and quickly ran back into the bushes. After some time, it came along with a bunch of small monkeys.

"Looks like you have a guest Austin," Jason said

"What...?" Austin was surprised as he was met with multiple eyes. "Oh no, now you all want a banana. I don't have any more." while looking at the monkeys, but the monkeys were rigid in their patterns. They sat in front of him, eagerly waiting for some food.

"Okay, let me find something for you...." Austin said again. He looked at his bag and found the peanuts jar he had brought and gave it to each monkey.

They all raised their hands and took the offering and ran.

"It's funny to watch Austin with the monkey..." Dalmar said

"Yeah, that's Austin," Jason responded.

They all had their food and went inside the water until their legs were half-submerged, washing their hands and face.

"Let's pack and leave now" Jason stated.

They all packed their stuff and started walking further. They walked for another 5 hours and suddenly they came to a place where they could see the sky completely, where no more tree branches lay above them. The entire area filled with trees has been chopped off, as though they have come to bare land.

"What happened here?" Jason asked Dalmar

"It is one of the biggest issues we have here. We hardly have much forestry in our country and most of them are due to geographical location and harsh conditions. We are cutting our forest, it is shrinking day by day, and on top of that we see some smugglers cutting down the trees even though it has been restricted.".

"What are they doing with those woods?"

"There is a huge market for carbon fossils in the

middle east, so the smuggler makes easy money by exporting them illegally even though it is banned."

"People have to understand the importance of nature and without it, we cannot exist."

"I guess, they will realize when there is no more and it is affecting their daily life," Austin responded.

"It's all about business and profit. And the world is blind in the face of money...." Dalmar said.

They all walked further for an hour or so until the sun went down.

"We should take rest for the night here" Dalmar stated

Jason and Austin looked around for a minute and agreed. They both started making a tent, while Dalmar went out to bring some wood to make a bonfire. After some time they were having their food sitting next to the bonfire and Austin gazed at the star counting each of them. They chatted for some time and went inside their tent to sleep.

Early in the morning, Austin was still in his deep sleep when somebody was kicking him to wake up. He was still in deep sleep and just turned sideways, his eyes closed. This time there was a harsh kick. Immediately he opened his eyes to see who it was. As he opened his eyes, he saw a strange man with a big knife in his hand looming a few feet away outside his tent. Austin suddenly shouted and woke up abruptly, calling Jason and Dalmar.

22

"Come out from your tent." the stranger's havoc voice called out.

Austin was still half-asleep, but his eyes began to expand wide. He noticed Jason and Dalmar already standing and encircled by the gang. Everyone has a weapon or a tool in their hands. They were the same smugglers who had been transporting wood through this region. They observed these three young men and began interrogating them as they passed by.

"Who are you guys? What are you doing here in the middle of the forest?" One of the leaders asked them.

"We are searching for someone who is in this forest," Dalmar responded.

"Who is it?"

"It's my girlfriend. She has been kidnapped by Abuddin" Jason responded.

"Who? Abuddin?" As they all chuckle and glance at each other, the man remarks sarcastically.

Apparently, they knew Abuddin. In fact, they did some illegal business with them.

All three couldn't do anything at that moment, since they weren't prepared. Instead, they just stood there, trying to figure out their next move.

"Please don't hurt us," Austin hesitantly said.

"We are not going to hurt you, but we are going to rob all your stuff though." the man chuckled, eyeing all the items.

Pointing at the tents, the man asked the other men to grab some stuff that may be used for them. Obliging, the men walked towards each tent and scavenged through the materials.

"Since I pity you, I'll give you a tip. Don't go- it's a death sentence. There are around 30 members guarding that place. But at night, only 5 people remain. So if you still want to risk it, I'd suggest going in at night." He said, before walking away into the woods with his gang right behind him.

"What are we going to do now? We don't have anything left to travel further." Austin expressed concern.

"It doesn't matter Austin, we can figure something out. We need to find Emma. Let's take what we have and go" Jason responded, grabbing some leftover items close to him.

"Look up there..." Dalmar said. He showed the branch of a tree where had hung his bag.

"For a safer purpose, I kept my bag over there at night. We still have a few things left..." Dalmar responded.

Dalmar climbed the tree and got his bag. They took all their stuff and started moving further.

They walked the entire day until the evening when they were met with a section filled with extremely wildlife inhabitants. They could hear the sounds of wild animals, so they made sure to walk quietly to avoid any conflicts. Austin was so afraid that he switched his position and came in the middle, while Dalmar was in the front and Jason at the back. As they walked a few miles, they came to a place where every few blocks they would see dead elephants

"Do you believe it is the similar situation that we saw yesterday in the bare land?" Jason said to Delmar.

"Yes, it's animal poaching. It's a big business here to use it for funding illegal activities." "Maybe it would have been the same extremist group that we are looking for..." Jason responded

"It shows to what extent a human being can go to hurt, not only their fellow members but to animals as well..."

"It's really sad to see so many dead elephants," Austin murmured, avoiding the gaze of death.

Dalmar went a little forward and leaned down to pray in his native language to one of the dead elephants. Both Jason and Austin joined him from the back and prayed for the animal souls.

They started walking further and came across a

man-made narrow path leading further down. They began traveling on that path, and within a few minutes, a Tiger appeared in the other direction. They all paused, unsure of what to do. Jason was in the lead, with Austin and Dalmar close behind.

"Oh, my god. I'm going to die today..." Austin murmured as his whole body was trembling.

"Don't move. Stick to the ground" Jason responded sternly.

Suddenly, the tiger turned his head, and his eyes sharpened at the boys. Everybody was still, waiting for who would make the next move. Jason was ready to fight back if the tiger attacked in order to save Austin and Dalmar. The tiger slowly started walking forward before it started running toward them. Jason took a knife from his pocket, holding it firmly. Dalmar held a hiking stick he had collected while walking, while Austin was murmuring to himself, holding Delmar's shoulder for dear life. It started increasing its speed, and the boys held onto their weapons fiercely when it abruptly stopped a few yards from them and ran away. Austin was happy thinking the tiger was afraid of him. But, suddenly all of them heard rustling behind them. As they all three turned back, they saw native tribes around 12 members holding some wooden weaponry. They weren't wearing any clothes, rather their bodies were covered up with leaves and black tribal marks. 5 men came forward and wrapped a hard leather material around their hands. Dalmar tried to talk to them but they pretended not to hear them.

"Where are they taking us?" Austin shouted

"They are taking us to their leader" Dalmar responded

"What are they going to do?"

"Not sure"

"Are they going to cook and eat us? I have seen it in some movies?" Austin expressed concern.

"Austin, be quiet," Jason said, thinking Austin may not be wrong.

After a few minutes of walking, they arrived at their place. The place looked like a small tribe and women doing some sort of artwork and children playing around. They are all wearing some sort of naturally woven cloth made of plants. They stopped right in front of the leader's mud hut house, one of the tribes went inside, and a few seconds later came up with the leader.

The leader was a wise man and he had a small crown made of plant leaves and bamboo. He was wearing a big necklace made out of animal teeth. He stood in front of Jason and asked in his native language.

"Who are you? What are you doing here in our territory?" He said flagrantly as he seemed to not know English well. He wanted to make sure they are not here to harm them.

Jason started speaking, "We are here trying to...." and stopped speaking since he understood they were not able to understand his language. Dalmar came forward and started speaking in their language.

"We are here to find his girlfriend who has been kidnapped by extremists."

The leader and Dalmar spoke for a few minutes in their language and the leader understood that they are harmless to their people, and allowed them to stay for tonight.

"The leader said we can spend the night and leave tomorrow morning," Dalmar told the other two.

"What? They are not going to kill us" Austin excitedly asked.

"No, they are friendly people. They just wanted to make sure, we didn't come here to harm them"

"I think, we should all stay here since it's already dark," Jason agreed

They all agreed to remain.. The leader told one of his men to show them the hut where they can stay and meet them during their dinner time. The men took them to show their hut. On their way, Jason and Austin were watching the activities that were happening outside at one of the sections. They saw the man lying down and one of the tribes trying to put some sort of paste on his body and using some sort of leaf wave on his body with some mantra in their language. When Jason asked Dalmar what's that all about.

"The man is hurt and he is healing that person."

"They don't take them to the hospital if they are badly hurt here?" Austin asked.

"No, there are no hospitals here. They are experts in their customs and they know what they are doing. It's a tradition to pass the skills from one generation to the next generation. It has been like that for many centuries. This is how they are able to live peacefully here without any connection with the outside world."

"Interesting... I have never met people who live like this..." Jason remarked.

They showed them the hut to stay in and they all went inside to take a rest. Some kids came to their hut and were looking at them and laughing at each other. Jason waved his hand and asked them to come here. They were giggling, still wondering what they were wearing and who they were. Austin took out some chocolates he had in his pocket and gave them. They came slowly walking in front of them and took those chocolates as if they had never seen chocolates before. Slowly they opened the wrapper and started tasting it. Initially, they didn't like the texture, but then the flavor exploded in their mouths, and felt it was magical. Austin started playing with them, meanwhile, Justin and Dalmar started to freshen up.

Later in the night, all the tribes gathered together in a place where they usually have their dinner surrounding a large fireplace. A few of them started singing and dancing, and one of the tribes pulled Jason and Austin and asked them to start dancing with them. Jason and Austin saw each other for a moment, thinking in their mind "whether we should join" they started mingling with them and started dancing. Dalmar was sitting next to the leader and watching them dance. An hour later, they started having dinner with lots of varieties of foods that they have never seen before.

"What is this?" Austin was hesitant at first.

"It's pretty much enriched cultural food, you may like it" Dalmar responded as Austin slowly started sipping the soup that they had made.

"Awesome, something different, I like it," Austin said with excitement, grabbing another spoonful.

After having dinner, they spoke for a few hours with the leader, and Dalmar translated the leader's words to Jason and Austin. "We were robbed by a group of poachers and lost all our weapons and equipment needed for the journey. Can we get some equipment and weapons to continue our journey?" Dalmar asked the leader.

"Of course....." The leader told one of his people to hand over some of the wooden weapons, ropes, and other necessary pieces of equipment in the morning. They all thanked the leader and their people and went to bed late at night.

The next fine morning, they all woke up and were ready to leave. Some of the members brought some of the items that they requested: ropes, a needle weapon to make the enemy unconscious, a bow, and an arrow. The leader came and wished them good luck in searching for their beloved friend.

"Thank you for all the hospitality that you and your people have provided," Jason said to them while Dalmar translated it to the leader.

"It is our honor and duty to serve guests with love

and compassion. It has been taught by our ancestors and we are just following their footsteps and customs." the leader responded smiling as he bowed his head.

"Such a profound tradition. I wish the entire world would have followed this. We would have been living peacefully and happily" Jason stated.

While Jason was talking to the leader, Austin was learning from one of the tribes how to use the weapon. He was struggling to hit the target, but the tribe patiently taught him, and finally. After a lot of struggles and hindrances, he learned to use it.

"Jason did you see that, I hit the target!!" Austin yelled excitedly to him.

"Let's go!!!!!" Jason yelled in response, giving Austin a fist bump.

They finally left and started heading in the direction that Dalmar had drawn on the map. They walked the entire day and came to a place where there were steep rocks.

"I think we need to climb this rock," Dalmar said, looking around to see if there was an alternative option to get across.

"Are you sure? Are you sure that this is the way...?" Jason questioned and he came closer to check the map that Dalmar was holding

"Yes, this is the place that the injured person had said."

Austin was a bit hesitant and was not trained for rock climbing as Jason had learned during his scout training.

"I cannot climb this rock. Look at me, do you think I can climb?" he gestured by waving his hands in the air.

"Don't worry buddy, I will figure out something," Jason responded.

They started climbing on rocks in the following minute. Both climbed effortlessly while holding tools and ropes, placing the appropriate hooks, and dragging Austin with a rope tied to him.

"Oh my God... Why am I here?" Austin froze while looking at the ground as Dalmar was holding him through the rope.

"Don't look down!" Dalmar shouted.

"Too Late!!" he quivered.

"Don't worry, he will be ok. We have to push him for a bit until he gets comfortable." Jason shouted as the wind was gushing them.

Finally, they were able to climb that rock and were able to bring Austin up as well.

"I survived!" Austin screamed, proud of himself.

They all laugh at each other. Later, Dalmar walked near the other edge with his binoculars scanning the area. He finally found the camp where extremists were holding the hostages.

"Look, come here guys. I can see the camps," Dalmar shouted.

Jason came running and took a binocular from Dalmar.

"Look in this direction," he pointed to the left.

Jason looked and could see a group of people

holding guns, guarding the surrounding perimeter. Later Austin came and evaluated the whole situation as well.

"Let me look," Austin asked Jason to hand over the binoculars.

Jason was now at ease and eager to meet Emma. They all made plans on how they needed to rescue her.

As suggested by the smuggler. "We should go in the night to rescue as there will be fewer people guarding. The rest will be sleeping." Dalmar said.

"Yeah, I agree with him..." Austin looked at Justin and stated.

"Ok, we will ambush at midnight."

They all sat and took some rest on the top of the rock until it was night.

23

It was midnight at 11 PM and Jason was standing, all geared up, looking through his binoculars and gazing at the camp from a mile away. The camp was dimly lit and it was powered by a loud generator. 5 soldiers were walking and holding their guns, guarding the entire perimeter of the camp.

"Are you guys ready?" Jason asked, while still holding the binoculars. They were both sitting, wearing armor and a blowgun containing a tranquilizer.

"Look, guys! I see only 5 soldiers. 2 of them are guarding a particular camp, where I think Emma is. The other 3 are taking turns walking the perimeter of the camp and the rest of the soldiers are sleeping in another building which is a few yards away." he bent down while stating to them.

"So what is the strategy?" Austin asked

"We all move in together. First take out those 3

soldiers and then attack the remaining 2 guards who are in front of the building" Jason responded.

"Ok, let's go then...," Dalmar said

"Are you ready Austin?"

"What am I doing here? Please never expect that I'll be fighting with a bunch of extremists in the middle of the jungle. Look, buddy. If I die during this battle, let my parents know I fought bravely till the end and never gave up." mockingly replied.

"Nothing is going to happen. Let's go."

They all started walking the narrow path, being very careful to make sure there was no grenade installed on the ground while walking every step. As they reached the boundary of the camp, they all sat near the boundary of the camp hiding behind the bushes.

Suddenly Austin stepped on a stone that started rolling making a descent noise that one of the soldiers who was walking nearby heard it. He started coming closer to the sound.

Austin in a low voice said "Guys I...."

Immediately Jason put his hand on his mouth indicating Austin to stop talking.

The soldier stopped and was gazing at the bushes for a few minutes to check if he still could hear any sounds. All three were status for a minute. The soldier didn't hear any sound, so he started turning back to go in the direction where he came from. Suddenly Jason jumped and held the soldier's mouth tightly with a piece of cloth having tranquilizer. Immediately the soldier fainted, and all three dragged him to the bush, Jason started wearing the soldier's clothes, with a cap and holding a gun.

"Wow, where did you learn all these tactics?" Austin asked.

"Remember when we were kids? I used to go to taekwondo. I asked you to join me but you said no."

"I regret that now."

"What would be the next move?" Dalmar asked Jason

"I'll start walking pretending to be their soldier. You guys follow me behind hiding, and when we get a chance we will knock down the other 2 who are walking."

Both of them lifted their thumb up and they all started walking openly. Jason was in the front with his cap down hiding his face, whereas Dalmar and Austin were hiding in the other corner. Another soldier started coming in front of Jason asking something, Jason started leaning down pretending to tie his shoes and the other soldier started asking in his language. Dalmar used a wooden blowgun and shot the needle on the soldier's neck. Immediately, the soldier rubbed his neck with his hand thinking it was a mosquito and fell down unconsciously. Jason immediately caught him, and they dragged him and hid him behind the bushes. They used a similar technique to the third soldier as well.

"2 more to go guys" Austin whispered.

"The 2 soldiers are right in front of the building.

Austin And I will attack from opposite sides using our blowgun. Dalmar, you go to the other camp and try to lock from outside so that the other soldiers who are sleeping won't come out" Jason said.

Dalmar went in the direction of the other building whereas Jason and Austin walked slowly behind the building, and they came near the corner. Jason signaled Austin through his hand to shoot a needle at the same time, he raised his hand and counted 1, 2 and 3. Jason shot the needle on his side of the soldier. The soldier immediately fell down, but Austin couldn't do it on time. He was still trying to blow, but it looks like the blowpipe didn't work, and he is trying to blow desperately again.

While the other soldier was puzzled why he fell down. He tried to put his hand to wake him up, Austin finally shot the needle and made the other soldier unconscious as well. They both ran and dragged the two soldiers near the bushes again, In the meantime, Dalmar came back after locking the door.

"Let's go inside." Jason murmured as he opened the door, he was surprised. Instead of Emma, they saw more than 30 prisoners occupied in multiple cells. Most of them were locals except a few.

Three of them looked at each other's faces, "Let's look at every cell." Jason said and started walking in front of the cell, calling for Emma while Austin did the same. All the prisoners started waking up. There were few noises and they started raising their hands on the bar, asking them to help them. Jason looked at Dalmar's face.

"They're local, from surrounding towns. If they don't agree to join their force, they would imprison them." Dalmar replied.

"Let's release them."

Dalmar started opening the cell lock and asked them to be quiet and showed them the way to the bushes. They all started opening each cell to release the prisoner while searching for Emma. Some prisoners started praising and some hugging these folks and left quietly heading towards the bushes. They opened almost all the cells except one. There was only one woman prisoner, still sleeping with her back turned . Finally, they were happy and Jason shouted "Emma!"

The girl turned where the voice was coming, as she turned, Jason and Austin were disappointed when they noticed her face. It was not Emma. It was some other girl. They opened the door and Jason rushed inside the cell.

"Have you seen Emma? He showed her a picture."

She was confused and surprised, and she had no idea what was going on. She saw all the other prisoners were escaping, she saw Jason's face again.

"Have you seen her?" Jason asked her again.

"Yes, yes, I've seen her," the girl replied.

"Where?".

"She was with me in this cell. We both were

together until this morning when they took her somewhere else."

"Where did they take her?"

"Not sure."

"We may have to enter the other camp and directly ask Abuddin" Jason restlessly said while looking at Dalmar and Austin.

"Are you sure? You want to enter that camp." Austin commented.

"All the other soldiers are inside that camp and they were sleeping along with his leader," Dalmar said

"There are no other choices, other than to enter that camp. If you have any other ideas let me know"

Both Austin and Dalmar looked at each other and nodded their head and said, "No"

"What about the girl?" Dalmar questioned

while Austin staring at her eyes "I don't think you belong here. Do you?"

"No, I was kidnapped and they brought me here. My name is Natalia and I'm from New Zealand."

"Let's go, we don't have much time. The soldiers will soon wake up. We can't take that risk..." Jason said in a hurry.

All four started going to the other camp. They slowly opened the locked door and as they entered, they saw all soldiers were in deep sleep and the leader, Abuddin, was sleeping inside a room alone. They slowly opened the room and Jason took one of their guns and pointed it at Abuddin's face to wake him up.

He abruptly opened his eyes, he started to yell, and they all hold their finger on his lips,

"Shhhhhhhhh" Jason said to Abuddin

"You people again. You guys followed me...."

"Where is Emma?"

"Why would I tell you?"

"Look, I have the gun and I won't hesitate to kill you if you don't tell me where Emma is..."

"Go ahead then, I don't care," Abuddin replied, smirking.

"I saw you making a deal while you were holding Emma as hostage." Natalia shouted at Abuddin face

"Oh, you saw that."

"Let's kill him. There is no point in keeping him alive. We will hold a soldier and ask him about Emma." Jason said angrily.

Dalmar rushed with a gun pointing at his head. They all pretended they were being serious, but rather they were bluffing. Abuddin began to think they were serious and began panicking.

"Alright, I'll tell you where she is...."

"Come on tell." Jason asked

"She was handed over to the Tafia today."

"Who is Tafia?" Austin shouted.

"Go ahead and ask your pal. He'd recognize Tafia." Abuddin pointed at Dalmar.

"Tafia is a Somali pirate. He lives in Xaafuun" Dalmar stated.

"Why would you hand it over to him?" Jason shouted at Abuddin

Abuddin was having a laugh and immediately Jason hit him with his rifle on his head. They all stopped Jason from hitting him further.

"I know why he would do that- for Money." Dalmar responded.

"Money, how would he get money from them?" Austin asked

"Usually Pirates are good negotiators. They know how to deal with companies and the government to get maximum money, so he would have traded Emma for money. Now, Tafia will be dealing with your government I think..."

"We have to chase him. If he leaves this morning, can we intercept somewhere in between?" Jason asked.

"No, usually they have pirate ships and travel through water to their place instead of land which is very dangerous for them." Dalmar replied.

"We have to leave immediately. Let's go."

"What about him?" Dalmar pointed at Abuddin

Austin places a handkerchief on Abuddin's nose, knocking him unconscious.

"All done!" Austin exclaimed, smiling.

They slowly started leaving the building from the back door.

"Wait. Wait... Let me take the keys to the truck" Dalmar said

As Dalmar took the shiny key that was lying on the table, he saw a bag filled with money.

"This is the money that he traded with Tafia! I think."

"We should take all this money. This would help in negotiating with the Tafia" Jason responded.

They took the bag filled with money and they left slowly one by one from the back door, heading towards the truck.

While traveling in the truck, Austin started conversation with Natalia

"How did you land here? how many days were you suffering?"

"I was a reporter and came to this country to cover a topic, but instead I was kidnapped by them. I may have to contact my editor once we reach Mogadishu."

It was pitch dark in the night and they were traveling alone in the truck heading towards the city.

24

When they arrived in Mogadishu after two days, a phone rang while they were at the hotel discussing their next step. Mike was on the other end.

"How are you, Jason?"

"I'm doing okay…"

"Did you find Emma?"

"No." Jason groaned.

"What happened?"

Jason started explaining the whole story of what occurred over the previous 5 days.

"Take it, easy. We will find Emma at any cost, no matter what level we need to reach to get attention."

"I'll be heading towards Xaafuun to find Emma."

"Before you head to Xaafuun, I want you to write the story you told me and send it over. We will publish and use this to get attention from the public and ultimately reach our leaders, enforcing them to take some action in finding Emma." Mike requested Jason.

"Is this necessary?"

"Yes, of course, otherwise, how are you going to negotiate with the Tafia? You know he is a pirate and what he needs is money. Our government has to step in to find any US citizen who is being held hostage in a foreign land."

"Ok, let me write it up and send it back to you before leaving Mogadishu."

"Look after yourself and Austin. Emma will be present when we chat again next time, hopefully." Mike said to him and ended the call.

"What happened?" Austin enquired

"Mike wants me to write an article about our journey and publish it so the public can help us."

"Yeah, Mike is right. We need as much sympathy as possible to find Emma."

"Okay, let me write it up tonight."

"Alright, You two take a rest, I'm going home tonight to see my family and will return tomorrow morning so we can drive to Xaafuun." Dalmar walked to the door and left the room.

Meanwhile, Jason sat with his laptop and wrote the entire story, and emailed to Mike. He was so exhausted that he collapsed on the couch and immediately fell asleep.

The next morning, Jason and Austin were browsing the internet to find out more information about the Tafia.

"I've found some information about Tafia from my source. He is not in Xaafuun. Instead, he took Emma somewhere in the middle of the Indian Ocean so that he could make better negotiations without any interaction with officials." Dalmar entered the room and eagerly said to them.

"He is very clever," Austin responded.

"He has dealt with many multinational companies by forcefully capturing their vessels. He knows what he is doing." Dalmar stated.

"We need to pinpoint the location and find a way to go there. Let's find a boat and start searching the ocean, he might not be that far from the land" Jason said to them.

"I know the location where he might have gone based on his past dealing."

"Let's pack and move. I wanted to bring Emma back safely as soon as possible."

"Wait, I need to check Natalia. I will be back" Austin left the room and went to the next room outside and knocked on the door.

Natalia approached the door and checked through the peephole before opening it.

"Hey, Austin. How are you doing?"

"I'm doing well. How is everything?"

"Pretty good. I had a nice sleep after a long time."

"Listen, we are checking out and heading to the ocean. So what's your plan?"

"I'm trying to contact my editor, but I'm not getting any response from him."

"Why don't you go to your Embassy and get help."

"There's no one there..."

"Oh," Austin sighed.

"Can I come with you guys then?"

"Yeah, but it's very dangerous. You will be safe here."

"Listen, it's not like I'm safe in the hotel either. Anybody can come and kidnap me again. After all of this, I don't think I can stay here. It's better to come with you guys."

"All right, pack your belongings and get ready. We're departing in 10 minutes." Austin stated. His cheeks were flushed as he exited the room. He began to feel a connection with Natalia.

They all checked out of the hotel and started traveling to a place where they could rent the boat.

"Are you sure you want to come with us, Natalia?" Jason asked.

"I'm damn sure" Natalia boldly responded.

Jason noticed Austin's eyes light up as he looked at her. Jason realized Austin had feelings for her.

"By the way, I forgot to ask you-how is your family Dalmar?" Jason asked while Dalmar was driving the car.

"They are doing well, pretty much busy with their usual daily routine. My younger sister is almost finishing her studies and writing her final exams. Hopefully, once she graduates, she will find a job and settle down."

"That's good. You have a nice family."

"Thanks. Trying our best to live in this chaotic world."

They all came to the docking place and spoke to one of the rental companies for a boat.

"Guys, this is the final call, it's not safe to travel further with me. If anybody wants to stay here, then say it now." Jason asked while watching everybody's reaction.

They looked at each other while thinking about whom he was asking. They started stepping inside the boat, while Jason was still waiting for their answer. He understood they had made up their mind. They started heading toward the East in the Indian Ocean.

New York.

While in the US, Mike has already published an article about the current status of Emma and Jason. The news had already spread all over the world. Emma's parents were worried and couldn't even go out, since they were surrounded by cameras. Furthermore, there was immense pressure on the government to take action. They're desperately working to find some sort of solution.

At the office, Mike was sitting in Paul's room. He was thoroughly pondering the entire circumstance and was worried owing to the critical situation. And they began talking about Emma's position.

"What do you think? Is this going to work?" Paul asked Mike.

"It should work. The recent article has opened up more pressure in the White House to come up with a rescue operation and bring our guys home safely. We need their help apart from the effort we are doing here."

"Was there any demand from the pirates yet?"

"Not yet, a call might come anytime. I'm not sure where it might ring."

While they were discussing for quite some time, suddenly a phone rang. They looked at each other, worried. Paul took the phone and it was his secretary on the other line.

"Paul, someone named Talmar from Somalia wants to talk to you." his secretary told him.

"Connect me," Paul signaled Mike.

He was anxious and he whispered through his facial expression to Mike that it was pirates and switched on the loudspeaker so that Mike could also hear.

"Am I talking to the president of Global world news?" the Pirate spoke with a harsh tone.

"Yes, this is Paul from Global world news. Who is this?" Paul said while Mike started focusing and concentrating on the voice.

"This is Tafia, the leader of the pirates. Emma is held as a hostage under my custody and I demand $100 million dollars for her release."

Paul didn't know what to say. Mike encouraged him that to ask how is Emma,

"Look, we need some time to think about it. First, we want to know that Emma is safe."

"Don't worry about Emma. She is fine with us as

long as you agree and give us the money in a week. I'll call you again tomorrow to know your answer." and hung up the phone.

Paul relaxed and was confused about what he had to do next.

"We should inform their parents that Emma is safe at the moment and let the Mayor knows about this phone call," Mike said

"Yeah what options do we have? I may have to arrange the money as well. Let me talk to the board members." Paul said in return.

"Let me make those calls," Mike said and left Paul's office.

He made phone calls to Emma's and Jason's parents and informed them and called the New York City Mayor specifying their demands. Jason's Dad informed his politician friend Brook and asked him to do something. Due to pressure from the public and media about the situation, the Mayor had an urgent meeting with his team. Brook was present as well. The mayor called Washington on a secured video conference, and every official present had the certain authority to make decisions.

"We came to know about Emma and the Pirates are asking for $100 million," Mayor stated at the conference.

There were few chit-chats between them

"We have to do something, the people have become serious and are asking questions on this matter," Brook added.

"Were there any other demands from them?" the homeland security from Washington asked through video chat.

"No, it was just money I think…." Brook responded.

"Mayor, let us get back to you after we discuss here." and the conference ended.

Everyone left the room, Brook held the mayor for a moment and said

"Are they going to take some action?"

"Let's wait and see what decision they make…."

"We don't have much time."

"I know, hopefully. Washington will come up with some tactical decisions fast. " the Mayor said in return.

25

Indian Ocean, near Somalia

Back in Somalia, Jason and the others have been in the ocean for 3 days searching for Emma.

"Jason, it's been 3 days now. We still can't pinpoint the location." Austin spoke sluggishly.

"We can't give up. We have to find Emma and rescue her."

They all kept searching the ocean, and at one point, they came to a place where there was trash all over the ocean. Due to the immense pollution in the water, the color of the water was dark and was killing millions of habitats.

"Can you smell the foul scent? Maybe it's coming out of the ocean.." Natalia said to them.

"The ocean is severely polluted by plastic, manufacturing, and petroleum waste. The water smells bad as a result of this." Dalmar told them.

"It appears that we as humans are planning ways to destroy the defenseless marine life," Jason added.

"Yeah, eighty percent of the marine pollution comes from the land, and the humans are behind it."

Everyone nodded their heads in disappointment before gearing into another conversation.

On the fourth night, everyone was chatting onboard when Dalmar suddenly saw a light outline of a boat emitting light. Immediately Dalmar asked Austin to turn off the engine and the light.

"Why, what just transpired?" Austin enquired.

Jason was looking in his binoculars to check whose boat it was.

"There's a boat," Dalmar said

"Where?" Austin asked again

Jason saw a few men standing on the boat with a gun. Immediately he said,

"I think we found them..." Jason said while still holding his binoculars.

He was looking to see if it was Tafia's boat. He was rotating his binoculars from left to right, up and down, searching every corner. Suddenly, he stopped and saw there was a girl in one of the rooms. He couldn't see her face but noticed her hair was black.

She even felt like someone was watching her, so she tilted her head to the side and gazed out the window.

" Guys! I found Emma!" Jason exclaimed

Austin snatched the binoculars and started looking. Jason was restless and eager to rescue Emma as quickly as he could.

"We need to come up with a plan. Does anyone have any suggestions?" Jason asked the group.

"We should give the money we collected from Abuddin," Austin responded.

"I don't think that will work out. Why would he take back his own money and hand it over to her?" Dalmar reasoned.

"So the only option is to rescue her," Jason replied.

"Yes," Dalmar said again.

"Let's wait until it becomes darker and move our ship closer to theirs." Jason specified as he took the binoculars to check how many men were there.

"There are 14 people. 2 are guarding Emma near the door. The rest are surrounding the boat. The only option I think would be to knock out the guards that are near Emma. We can't reasonably fight all 14 of them, so we must be quiet."

"The boat sound may alert them so we will stop our boat at a certain distance and swim over there" Dalmar added.

" I agree..." Jason replied.

"I get to use the blowpipe again!" Austin grinned as he reached and held the blowpipe.

"Let's gear up and be ready to jump when we are closer" Jason stated before getting ready himself.

Emma was exhausted and quite pale in the Tafia boat. She was contemplating what may occur to her next. She didn't think her company would pay the amount because she had just joined the firm. Could Jason be looking for me? Am I going to die? Multiple scenarios played out in her thoughts as she pondered incoherently.

"Boss, should we take a rest? It's night. I doubt they'll deliver us the money at this time." one of the gang members asked.

"Be on guard. We can never predict what they'll do. Keep in mind that underestimating someone will be our downfall. " Talmar sternly said to them.

"Do you think they are going to pay us the money?"

"You tell me. Have we ever not gotten what we wanted?"

"We've always been successful."

"If you know the answer, then why are you asking me then?" Talmar stated, looking into the wavering ocean. "This time, the matter has become very serious. Everyone across the globe is aware of this girl. We will either come out of this scenario rich or dead. Considering what happened to the other group last year, I'm particularly concerned. They were captured and killed. However, they lacked a leader like me. I have kept you guys alive for many years, and I'm determined to keep that true." Tafia was leaning on the boat and facing his member when he saw his gang member's eyes wide open,

"What Happened?" Talmar asked

His gang member was speechless. He turned his face to the ocean and he saw a submarine emerge out of the ocean approximately half a mile from their boat. They were shocked.

"Everyone be alert!" Talmar ordered, carefully examining where the submarine was.

He never expected he was going to deal with the US military, his negotiations have never been this much of a serious matter. All the gang members were worried.

In the submarine, the captain and his team came out with binoculars and looked at the situation. Apparently, a US official in Washington contacted the captain and rerouted them here to handle the situation. The captain used a loudspeaker connected to the submarine to give the pirates a warning.

"Release the hostage or we will come and shoot at you" the captain ordered.

Emma's release would have a negative impact on Tafia's reputation and, more crucially, his legacy in general. He decided not to give up Emma at any cost.

26

As everyone was about to initiate their plan, Jason was surprised to see a large submarine.

"They heard our story! The U.S. government sent a rescue mission to save Emma!" Austin yelled with a smiley face.

"Look, we don't have much time. This is the perfect opportunity to jump now while they're all distracted. The last thing they'll expect is for us to ambush them as well." Jason responded

"Why? The marine is more than capable of rescuing Emma." Austin responded.

"No, it can go wrong anytime. We don't know if they are here to negotiate with the pirates and they might jeopardize Emma's life. We need to go now." Jason reasoned. "Dalmar gets some extra gear for Emma. We are jumping now- Natalia, you control the boat and stay here."

Dalmar brought the extra gear, while Austin got ready with his blowpipe.

"Let's go guys," Jason said and jumped in the water with Dalmar right behind him. Austin looked at Natalia.

"Be careful?" Natalia stated while displaying concern on her face.

"Of course," Austin replied. He wanted to kiss her, but he wanted to wait for the right moment. Smiling back at her, he turned around and jumped off the boat.

Everyone was impacted by the freezing temperatures of the cold ocean, but they knew nothing could stop them from continuing on. Swimming slowly, they made their way to Tafia's boat. They decided to swim toward the back of the boat where most of the gang members weren't present. Slowly they climbed up a small sliver ladder and crouched behind a large box that lay a few feet in front of them. They noticed only one person blocking the steps that reached Emma's room. Jason signaled Austin and pointed at the stationary man. Austin grinned and pulled out the silver weaponry and with the smallest blow of air, the needle pricked the man's neck. The man, noticing something hit him, touched his neck when he noticed the boys. As he was about to say something, he began feeling drowsy and touched his head. He slowly lowered his body to sit on the step until the drug took its full effect and knocked him unconscious. Austin was very excited that it worked in one shot.

"Did you see that?" Austin whispered happily.

Jason raised his fingers to his mouth, signaling Austin to be quiet. But Austin saw Jason smile in acknowledgment, so he happily nodded and focused back on their main goal. Jason looked around the area to ensure no one was looking as he slowly reached the steps and climbed up.

"We will give you one hour to send her back to us. Otherwise," there was a pause. "Just wait and see." You could almost hear the smirk that expelled the speaker from the captain of the submarine.

The gang members began pointing guns at the submarine, waiting for the Tafia's response. As that was continuing on the first floor, Jason and Dalmar are on the top floor, knocking out the remaining 2 who were in Emma's room. While Austin was at the foot of the stairs, watching outside, Jason and Dalmar entered the room.

"Jason..." Emma was shocked to see him, she whispered before running towards him and giving him a tight hug.

Jason tightened his grip after experiencing a tremendous feeling of relief.

"Guys, guys. We need to get out of here." Austin appeared at the door.

"I never expected you to rescue me," Emma spoke softly.

"How could I not? You're a part of my life now" Jason responded.

Emma looked at Dalmar and then at Austin and smiled.

"You look pale and sick" Austin looked at Emma and hugged her.

"I will be fine."

"We should make our way back now," Dalmar said and gave her the extra gear they got with them before leading them out of the room.

"He is our friend- Dalmar. He assisted us in locating you. We wouldn't have progressed this far without him." Jason stated

While the gang was still preoccupied with the marine, they carefully made their way downstairs and jumped into the ocean one by one, and slowly started heading towards their boat.

They reached and Dalmar took control of the boat and started heading toward the submarine in a circle. Emma couldn't believe that she was finally rescued by her beloved. She stood next to him while he was cruising, holding him.

Back on the submarine, the soldiers were ready to take clear shots at the pirate's ship, just waiting for the Captain's order.

"This is your final warning. Let the hostage be released. Otherwise, we will start shooting." the captain warned again.

The pirates took their position to defend themselves without being aware that Emma had already escaped.

While the captain was ready to order his soldier, suddenly one of the soldiers noticed that there was another boat coming from behind the submarine.

The pirates, thinking it was more military, began panicking and started to speed away from the ships. Unfortunately, they didn't realize their hostage wasn't on board until it was too late.

The soldiers started pointing guns in both directions, while the captain turned and looked through his binoculars and saw a boy waving the American flag. The captain was surprised and immediately asked his soldiers to hold down their guns. As the boat was approaching, it was clear that Emma had escaped from the pirates. They came closer to the submarine.

"Are you Emma and Justin?" the captain asked.

"Yes," Jason responded.

"We rescued Emma from the pirates," Austin told them proudly.

"Good work young man. You saved some lives today." the captain proudly said over the speaker. Suddenly there was a clicking sound and a huge release of air appeared to be released above the submarine.

"Come on board the submarine, everyone. We'll take you home." the captain said to them.

Austin asked Natalia to join as well. She was happy to be with Austin.

"Dalmar, this is it. Thank you for all your support. We are never going to forget what you have done for us." Jason said

"As promised, here is $10,000" Jason gave and hugged him.

"Thank you. I will miss all of you. Next time we

meet, let's try not to be in danger." Dalmar jokes.

Austin had a small tear in his eyes. He came and hugged Dalmar. "Can't make any promises."

Emma also came in front of Dalmar and expressed her gratitude for helping her. Slowly they started to descend into the submarine until Jason was the only one left.

"Wait, what should we do with this $1 million?" Dalmar asked.

"Keep it, you know what to do," Jason said and boarded the submarine.

"Be safe Dalmar!" Austin screamed from within the submarine.

"Take care, everyone, bye." Dalmar waved his hand and started driving in the opposite direction, heading toward his home.

The captain asked one of his soldiers to inform Washington that the mission ended not only successfully, but without any violence.

Tafia recognized right away that they had let them go free. He instructed one of his gang members to check Emma upstairs out of suspicion. The man ran upstairs and noticed the soldiers that were knocked out and the empty room. He came out shouting,

"Boss! Emma is missing- she has escaped."

Tafia fell on his chair and put his hand on his head, trying to digest and figure out what just happened.

On the other side, the two lovers had recently reconnected and were falling more and more in love with each other.

27

When they went inside the submarine, all the soldiers clapped and greeted them.

"Show them their room Soldier" The captain commanded one of his soldiers.

"Yes, Captain..."

The soldier gave them blankets and took them to a room where they could stay for the rest of their journey. Jason and Emma occupied cabin 1 whereas Austin and Natalia were in the cabin next door.

"You all can relax here. If you need anything else just do let me know as I'm outside." The soldier said to them before leaving.

Jason and Emma changed out of their wet clothes and wore military clothing that was lying on the bed. Emma leaned on Jason's chest.

"I never expected you to rescue me, Jason."

"Why would you think like that? I cannot abandon

you after all the troubles we have gone through together." Jason said to her.

"So sweet of you, Jason. You've changed a lot since I first met you. I've never explicitly told you that I love you." she said before placing a soft long kiss on his lips.

"You know, I have felt the same for you since the day I saw you first"

Emma began laughing.

"I'm being serious." Jason expressed his feeling "You know, every time I'm with you, I feel like I'm the luckiest person in the world. I can't believe I get to wake up next to you finally."

"I feel the same way. You make my life so much brighter, and I love everything about you. Your laugh, your courage to find me, the way you look at me - it all makes me feel so loved."

"I want to spend the rest of my life making you happy. You deserve the best of the world, and I'll do everything I can to make sure you have it."

"You already make me the happiest person in the world, just by being here with me. I don't need anything else as long as I have you by my side. I love you more than anything." she kissed him again.

"I'm so excited to go home..."Emma exclaimed, and crushed herself on the bed.

"They told us we have 2 days to reach New York."

"What are we gonna- wait, we should go explore. I've never been on one of these" Emma said curiously.

"Before we start exploring the submarine, tell me what happened after Abuddin took you."

She then started explaining her story and Jason listened intently. On the other side of the wall, Austin and Natalia were discussing their feelings for one another as they gazed out the window to see the dark ocean, while the submarine was heading to its destination New York City.

After 2 days of journey, the submarine arrived at Battery Park, New York city. The captain and the soldiers came out initially, and later, all 4 of them came out wearing the marine dress they were given.

As they stepped out, they were surprised to see so many people welcoming them. They had no idea there would be so many people waiting for them and welcoming them. While they were escorted to the car, the new reporters started asking questions. Jason and Emma stopped for a minute. Jason had a responsibility to answer some of their questions since it was because of them, that he was able to save Emma.

"Jason, how do you feel now after finally getting Emma back?" one of the reporters asked.

"I feel very happy that we are back safely after going through all the trouble we had," Jason replied.

"Emma, are you in love with Jason?" another reporter asked.

She smiled while looking at Jason.

"I want to express my gratitude to everyone around the nation. We were able to come home safely thanks to your assistance." Emma said to the news reporters.

While the reporters were still asking questions, they had already reached the car and headed towards their respective homes, while Austin took Natalia to his apartment.

When they reached, Jason's mother abruptly went outside of her house after listening to the news of the arrival of her son. Her heart was pounding fast as she was desperate to see his son. When Jason came, she felt the life inside her body rise again. Emma's parents, on the other hand, were thrilled to see their daughter return home safely after a few months.

28

It's been a few weeks, and they all have been relaxing at their respective homes. One fine day, Jason woke up and dialed Austin's cell phone. He was still in bed, fast asleep, and ignored the phone ringing. Jason thought that it would be better to grab him from his apartment. He quickly brushed his teeth, showered, and ate a quick breakfast before leaving to pick Austin up from his apartment.

The doorbell started ringing continuously until Natalia woke up.

"Austin, wake up, wake up. There is someone at the door."

Austin was still asleep and was not waking up. She then went and opened the door.

"Good morning Natalia. Where is Austin?" Jason asked.

"He is still sleeping, I woke him but he ignored me."

"Let me wake him up."

"Wake up buddy. Wake up...." he shook him forcibly

"Jesus! What happened?" Austin was still yawning and talking in a slow-motion voice

"Come on, get ready. We need to go."

"Wait! What? Where are we going?"

"I'll tell you on the way."

"Jason, tell me where..."

"There is no time. I'll tell you on the way."

"Okay, let me go to the restroom and get ready. Give me 20 minutes." he was still yawning and talking.

"Alright, come fast. I'll be in the living room" Jason said, before heading in the opposite direction.

In the meantime, Natalia asked Jason for breakfast as she was going to prepare breakfast for everyone.

"No, I'm good. I just had breakfast at home. I wouldn't mind some coffee though."

"Coming right up!." Natalia said while having a smile on her face.

She started preparing the coffee and gave it to him. They both sat at the breakfast table and started talking with each other.

"Can I ask something?" Natalia asked Jason

"Sure. Go ahead...."

"What's so special today? I mean, I can sense your energy today...." Natalia was saying and Jason interrupted her.

"Today I'm going to propose to Emma to marry me."

"That's so sweet!! You guys deserve happiness." Natalia screamed with excitement.

"I have to find her a ring right away."

By the time, Austin came out and he was all dressed up.

"Austin, I need to tell you this, your friend is proposing to Emma!" In a rush, Natalia uttered

"What?? Dude, are you serious? I can't believe this. Are you settling down?" Austin simultaneously expressed delight and shock in his speech.

"Yes, I'm very serious. And this time I'm truly serious. Do you know when Abduddin kidnapped her and she was away from me? I felt jeopardized. For the first time in my life, I yearned for someone and was desperate to have her in my life. My heart was gonna explode with pain if I was unable to find her. At that point, I decided whenever we were out of the situation, I'm gonna make sure I'll always be there to protect her."

"That's good news. And I'm happy for you, buddy." Austin smiled and nodded his head.

"Let's go to the store and pick up a ring."

"Wait, let me have my breakfast" Austin groaned as his stomach grumbled in response.

"Hurry up, Austin."

He started having his breakfast while he was staring at Natalia. Austin was a little perplexed by his relationship with Natalia. He was staring at her and he could feel the strange sensations in his heart while looking at her.

"Natalia, do you want to join?" Austin asked her while holding her hands.

"No, you guys carry on. Have a good time, I've got some work to do."

Austin finished his breakfast and kissed Natalia.

"I will be back soon. Take care of yourself."

They left the apartment and reached the mall. Jason was assessing the jewelry stores while they were both strolling through the mall. He desired an elegant ring that would fit her personality. As they carried on with their shopping, Austin was munching on a pretzel with one hand.

"What is your plan dude?" Austin asked while still stuffing the pretzel in his mouth.

"I'll be proposing to Emma when I find the right time. Right now all I need is a simple elegant ring"

"My buddy is getting married! Soon he will be having his own family" he joked, jerking Jason's shoulder as they entered the Jewelry shop in the mall.

One of the saleswomen welcomed them,

"Can I help you sir?" the saleswoman asked them.

"My buddy is getting engaged. He is looking for a proposal ring. Do you have something elegant?" Austin asked the saleswoman.

"I can help you with that. Let me take a look around."

She opened the glass door of the display table and took out a few diamond rings.

"Here are the few finest diamond rings." She took

out some of the elegant rings and showed them to them.

Jason started looking at each of them and trying to see the design

"Are you looking for a specific ring sir?"

"I just need one simple single-stone diamond ring."

She took out a few more diamond rings and showed him.

He liked one of them and started evaluating the design of the ring. For a moment he imagined Emma and a ring on her hand and observing the ring on the basis of his fantasy.

"What do you think about this Austin?"

He looked at the ring, "It's good, simple, and pretty."

"Yeah, this is what I think Emma will like. It will look great on her."

"Do you know your partner's ring size sir?"

They looked at each other and were stunned. They both forgot about that.

"No, maybe. How can I forget about it?" Jason looked around and suddenly he observed the hands of the saleswoman. He realized that it was similar to Emma and he could use that as a reference.

"Her size is similar to your size. Maybe, if you don't mind, could you wear it and check whether it fits in your hand" Jason asked her.

The saleswoman took the ring and wore it.

"It perfectly fits me, sir. I think it would be great for her."

"Good, what is the price of this?" Austin inquired.

She saw the price tag and told them about the price of the ring.

"It's $5200, sir."

"Alright, please pack this." Jason requested.

"Of course." She packed the ring and gave it to them. Jason took his wallet and paid with his card and they both headed home.

Jason came to Austin's apartment to drop him off. Natalia was done with her paperwork and was applying for a visa to stay in the US until she travels back to New Zealand.

"Did you purchase the ring, Jason?" Natalia excitedly asked.

"Yes, of course. My buddy is getting engaged," Austin responded. Jason with a smile opened the packet and showed the ring to Natalia.

"So pretty, I'm sure Emma will love it."

"I hope so," he responded with a smile.

"When are you going to propose to her?"

"When the time is right, I'll propose to her..."

"And when is it, dude?" Austin made a sarcastic face and asked him.

"It will be anytime, Austin," Jason said to him while holding his arms tightly.

"Dude, after seeing you, I don't think you have to wait. Please propose to her as early as possible."

"Of course, I will be doing it pretty soon," he said to them and left their apartment.

29

They were all planning to go to the office today. Austin was getting ready while Natalia was revamping all of her pending tasks. Austin came near to her and pulled her in for a kiss.

"I'm going to the office now. I'll be back soon."

"It's already noon, Austin. Do you want to go to the office at this time?"

"Yes, just for a short time. We didn't go to the office after coming back. You may go for a walk in the city center if you feel bored. If you want to contact me on a cell phone, here is one."

"Don't worry about me. I've plenty of things to do. I will be fine."

Austin stopped for a minute and started looking at her without saying anything. He was holding her hands and looking at her face.

"Natalia, I'm in love with you. You should stay here in the city instead of going back to New Zealand.

Maybe it's grotesque that I'm saying it like this without arranging a special dinner for you. But I wanted to say it… "

She didn't say anything for a while until finally, a soft smile lit her face.

"If you're smiling, that means yes. You will be staying here?" he asked.

"I love you too. Let me think about it for some time," she said to him perplexed, dealing with her own conflicted situation.

A phone rang abruptly and it was Jason.

"I'm here. Can you come down buddy?"

Austin gave a kiss to her and left. Downstairs outside, he saw Jason and Emma chatting, holding each other like love birds. He was wondering whether he had already proposed to her or not.

"Hey, buddy, Hey Emma. You look good today. Just like Emma in old times." Austin said to her.

"Good morning Austin…" she smiled

He gave a look at Justin and without making any sound, silently mouthed if he proposed to her yet. Justin immediately asked him to keep his mouth closed for now and his face became flustered with nervousness.

"What's going on? You too are behaving weird" she remarked, glancing back and forth between them.

"Nothing, you know him. He is always like this, behaving like a buffoon." Jason responded.

He sat at the back in the car and they started heading to the office. While Jason was driving, he noticed Emma was so happy. Austin was very curious to find out the main reason for Emma's happiness.

"Why are you all excited?" Austin chuckled as he asked.

"It's been a long time since we've been to the office all together" she looked at Jason and smiled. Holding one of his hands, she placed a light kiss on his hand.

"Wow, look at you two. You both are meant to be with each other. I'm happy for both of you." Austin sweetly said to them.

"By the way, how is it going with you and Natalia?" she asked

"It's good. I like her very much. She is not only sweet, but she also has a perfect personality." Austin said with a twinkle in his eye.

"Looks like Austin is also in love." Emma teased.

"Yeah, fortunately, I am…."

All three were radiating love and their entire drive was pleasant. They finally reached the office and while looking at the office building they were reminiscing the old memories and had nostalgic feelings.

"Finally, we are back in the office." Jason proudly stated and they went inside. They took one of the elevators to the 30th floor and as they came out of the elevator, they were surprised. The entire team had stood up as they were waiting for them to arrive, and welcomed them with their welcoming gestures.

They never expected this surprise. Mike came in front of them and said

"Welcome back Jason and Emma!" and he hugged them.

Paul shook his hands with them as everyone around them was still clapping. Steve and Jessica came forward and hugged them as well. Right behind them, there were some tables arranged. Mike asked Jason and Emma to sit there as he went towards the microphone and asked everyone to be quiet before he started his speech.

"Welcome, Jason and Emma for your safe return. Although I could never understand the feeling you went through on your journey, I do know for a fact that you have touched millions of hearts across the world through the events that took place. We never expected your job would turn out like this. We are so proud of you two to be back and alive, and in fact, it has indirectly helped this company's stock to grow tremendously because of your story. Paul has suggested giving a bonus to everyone at this month's end for their hard work by helping to cover the story, while the whole world's camera was pointing at us."

Meanwhile, Paul made a successful gesture to his employee.

"Before I forget, I would also give special thanks to Austin for volunteering, even after knowing it was dangerous and bringing them safely home."

Austin felt so proud, he looked at his fellow coworkers and smiled.

"I would like now for Jason and Emma to come here and talk about their journey and add anything to this speech!" He smiled, gesturing towards them both.

Jason got up and came in front of the microphone.

"I'm very thankful for your support and bringing up our story to the world- it has helped us come home safely. The trip was supposed to be a fun experience, but it turned out to be quite the opposite. I never thought that my life would turn out like this. It changed my perspective completely in the past few months. Life dragged us into different conflict situations throughout the journey. We saw horrific incidents yet met many beautiful souls on the path, whom we will never forget. I'm just grateful for all of you guys, and I'm glad to be a part of this family."

Everyone was touched by his speech and clapped for him. Jessica asked Emma to talk about something even though Emma was not ready.

"Emma! What's your story?" Jessica asked, encouraging the crowd to support her question.

"Yes, Emma. Let us know." the crowd asked.

Emma walked slowly to the microphone

"Hey, everyone, I think Jason has covered most of the things that I wanted to say. The only thing I can add up about the situation is when they kidnapped me. I never thought that I would be alive and at one point, I'd given up hope about my life after going through and watching those horrible things that human beings can do to one another. While trapped, I met another girl, Natalia, who was from New Zealand. She had also been kidnapped and kept apart from other local hostages. We were supporting each other, and that gave us some hope to be alive. In fact, we planned and attempted to escape many times but we failed over and over again. That is when we gave up and left fate to decide our future. And it turned out to be Jason and Austin to rescue us. I never expected Jason to not give up on me."

Jason smiled while sitting at a distance. By the way, Natalia is Austin's girlfriend now..." Emma told the audience.

Austin smiled, and everyone cheered him. Austin was blushing while the whole audience was cheering for him.

"Thank you all for your support and to the entire world for helping us out." she smiled and started walking while Mike came and took the microphone and said,

"Enjoy the rest of the day, have fun and let's party!" Mike said and left the microphone. The colleagues stopped working and started to chat in the office. The music was turned on and was vibrating through the floors. Each team came and congratulated Jason, Emma, and Austin including Matt, Jessica, and Steve.

"Congratulations! It's good, you guys are back. We will be having a lot more fun while working together." Matt shook his hand with Jason.

"Thanks, Matt, we never expected you to support us like this..." Jason stated

"We don't care about our rivalry anymore, what

matters the most is you guys are back home safely" the rest of the gang nodded their heads.

While they were talking, Mike joined and asked Emma to accompany him in having a discussion with Paul. While Emma left with Mike, Austin started saying,

"Come on dude. You need to propose to her. This is the right time."

"What, what's going on here?" Matt asked.

"Our friend is thinking of proposing to Emma."

"Wow, that's lovely!" Jessica responded

"Our friend is getting engaged!" Matt stated.

"Yeah, I'm proposing to her today, but I'm waiting for the right time."

"I think, as Austin said, this is the right time. You should do it now." Matt suggested.

"No, this place is extremely crowded and noisy. I like to be in a quieter, place."Jason responded.

"Oh, in that case, take her out for dinner at a nice restaurant and propose," Austin replied.

"Yeah, that's a good idea," Jessica said

"Yes, you should do that." Matt and the rest of them nodded their heads as well.

"That's not a bad idea. I'll do that." Jason smiled and blushed.

By the time Emma arrived everyone was acting suspiciously. She evaluated the whole situation and her spider-sense was always telling her that something is going on with them. She asked everyone,

"What's going on here?"

"Nothing, just chatting. Just talking about work." Austin replied, slowly he and the rest of the folks began slipping away, leaving the two of them alone.

"What happened to them? Why do they leave us alone?" Emma asked

Jason gave a smile and looked at her. His heart was pounding fast and he had an immense feeling for Emma.

"Let's go for dinner. It's been a while since we went out together in the city." Jason asked her.

"What? Right now? And what about all of them? They were all here for us."

"They are busy and having fun. I'm sure they'll be fine with Austin. Don't worry and let's go…"

She smiled and nodded. "Alright, let's go."

The rest of the gang saw them going. Austin gave a gesture with his hand pulling down his right hand and saying,

"The couple is leaving!" he made eye contact with Jason and made a gesture.

30

They both entered a nice Italian restaurant in front of time square. Emma was looking charming in her casual dress. She had sophisticated, stylish pointed cinder gray shoes and a matching bag- she was looking exceptionally gorgeous. On the other hand, Jason was dressed in a sophisticated three-piece he had worn from a meeting. His gray slacks, black slim-fit tie, and white shirt contemplated his blue eyes. However, his skin poking out from the collar of his shirt was always a treat.

"How can I help you, sir? Do you want a table for two? " the receptionist asked.

"Yes," Jason responded

"Do you have a reservation, sir?"

"No. I didn't have any reservations. But please make it special, if possible, even with such short notice."

"Of course, I'll be right back." She went to check the tables and returned.

"Usually we don't have empty tables, but you are lucky. Today to have a table and it's right next to the window with a mesmerizing view of Times Square…" the receptionist smiled

"We'll take it, thank you so much."

She took two menus and asked them to follow her. She showed them the table and said

"Enjoy your dinner." She handed over the menu and left.

They both sat facing each other with a big window on the side. The glass was tinted, but they could see the busy city with people walking around, taking pictures. They both felt the view was beautiful in the presence of each other.

Jason continued looking at Emma, thinking about how gorgeous she seemed tonight. Jason caught Emma's attention as well, and she smiled as she noticed how attractive he was. She experienced a strong sense of safety and joy and realized she genuinely loved him.

A waitress came in front of their table.

"Hello, my name is Gail. I'll be serving today for the lovely couples. What would you like to drink sir?" she asked them with a smiling face.

Jason looked at the drink menu

"Would you like to have a wine?" he asked Emma,

"Sure."

He looked at the wine section, there were many choices to choose from

"Can we get 2 glasses of *Chateau Lynch Bages Pauillac, 1995?*" Jason asked her.

"That's a good choice, sir. I'll be back soon..." and she left.

Emma was surprised that he ordered the most expensive wine and was curious about what was going on with him. He was acting differently than usual.

"That's pretty expensive. I really don't mind what we drink- you don't need to impress me. I've already swooned." Emma jokingly said to him.

He smiled, "It's our first dinner together after all those troubles, I think we both deserve this."

She held his hands and said, "I love you so much for not giving up on me. I don't know how I found you in my life, but I am forever grateful. The person who risked his life for me." Both were holding hands and staring into each other's eyes. Jason came near to her and gently held her chin up to kiss her. She kissed him deeply while there was a piece of background music playing. It was Mozart – Eine kleine Nachtmusik composed by Wolfgang Amadeus Mozart in 1787.

Jason was in the cloud nine. His cheeks turned completely red and he was glowing. Soon later, the waitress came and she saw them. She felt so touched by seeing them as she wished that she could find a partner to love her like that.

"Here is the wine bottle..." She interrupted, pouring the wine in front of them and handed over the glass of wine,

"Enjoy your drink you two..." she said with a smiling face

"What would you like to have for an appetizer sir?"

"We would like to start with Risotto, and a Roasted Tomato Bruschetta with a salad on the side."

" Thank you, I will be back soon" and she left again

They both took the wine glass and Jason made a toast.

"For our lovely moment together." They both laughed and smiled.

She smiled and drank the first sip and noticed that it had all four well-balanced tastes sweet, sour, salty, and bitter. It was the finest wine she had ever tasted. Along with the relaxing music, she felt this was the best date, and felt alive after a very long time. She was experiencing magical feelings that were pulling her toward Jason's direction. She felt she had finally found the right man for her.

While she was enjoying the wine, her eyes glazed outside the window and saw a couple with a baby happily taking pictures in front of time square.

"Look at that couple with baby, Jason. They're so adorable and look how happy they are..." Emma glanced at them.

He looked outside and noticed it. He was observing the cute smile on her face. Her adorable smile made Jason fall for her again and again.

"A very happy and adorable couple like us. Isn't it?" She teased.

He smiled and he felt that it was time to take out his ring. She interrupted and said

"Let me go to the restroom. I will be back" and she left with her purse.

While she went to the restroom, a sound came from his phone. It was a text message from Austin.

"Dude, did you propose?" Austin asked with his mere curiosity

"Not Yet. I will be doing it in a minute."

While he was still texting, Emma was looking at herself in the mirror in the restroom. She was trying to make her hair straight, putting foundation on her face and blush on her cheeks, and making sure she looked beautiful. She was so happy that she never felt like this before in her life. Is it because of the love she was thinking of? Later she came out of the restroom and started walking toward the table.

Jason noticed that Emma was coming, and he immediately texted his goodbyes.

While she was in front of the table, trying to sit, Jason said

"Wait, don't sit. I want to say something."

She was surprised that he was acting weird and she was looking around at the people in the restaurant.

He stood from his chair and kneeled in front of her. He slowly put his hand in his pocket and opened the box to show the ring.

"Emma, I never imagined meeting someone like you and falling in love. Although we've only known one other for a few months, it feels like we've known each other forever. Although the journey we had was terrifying, it also drew us much closer. I made the conscious decision to control my own destiny because I cannot fathom living life without you. Will you marry me?" he said and started eagerly waiting for Emma's reaction by watching her face.

Emma's face lit up, but just as she was about to respond, a bullet zipped through the air, smacking and shattering the glass window. Jason turned his head, following the sound and looked at the window for a second, the next thing he noticed that the bullet had already pierced Emma's head next to her right eye, causing blood to stream down. She briefly glazed over at Jason, and as he continued to do so, she started falling to the ground. Jason sprang to her side and tried to cradle her in his arms, he grabbed her just on time, but just as he was ready to react, she began to gradually close her eyes. Her heartbeat stopped and her pulse was nowhere. He can feel her skin in his hand but not her soul. There was a darkness that echoed into his heart and spread through his body. He screamed and paralyzed, still holding her in his arms and staring at the love of his life.

COMING SOON

Book - 2

Comments : Go to contact page in https://livinglibrarian.com

www.ingramcontent.com/pod-product-compliance
Lightning Source LLC
LaVergne TN
LVHW041632060526
838200LV00040B/1555